WILLIE ANDERSON

RAY SOWELL

authorHOUSE®

AuthorHouse™
1663 Liberty Drive
Bloomington, IN 47403
www.authorhouse.com
Phone: 1 (800) 839-8640

Published by AuthorHouse   08/04/2016

ISBN: 978-1-5246-2197-1 (sc)
ISBN: 978-1-5246-2196-4 (e)

Library of Congress Control Number: 2016912295

Print information available on the last page.

Around the turn of the century the Indians were going here and there trying to find a suitable place to live or as we would say to pitch their tent. The government was working up a plan to move them to certain reservations throughout the United States so they would have their own grounds that they could hunt on and not be bothered by any other tribe, but this was still a little ways off, so they Indians were doing the best they could at the time.

At this time the Hopi tribe did not have no help from the government whatsoever. They had to depend on their own hunting to find meat and food for their people. The meat was very scarce in this part of the southwest. Most of the buffalo had been killed off and the deer was getting pretty slim also.

The Indians knew that someday they would be moved to their own land but did not know to where that would be. They were hoping that it would be in and around the place that they were at. Now they only moved to the desert in the winter and then to the forest that was close to the river so they could get fish to eat then. That was almost all the meat that they could get now and that was the fish out of the river.

They only moved to the desert in the winter so they would not have such winter weather. They could still go to a forest and find the nuts that they made meal and flour out of. Vegetables in the winter was a scarce thing so they had to find the roots of some of the plants to eat. In the winter time this was getting worse every year until they moved in the spring.

Living in one of the tepees on the reservation was a middle age lady by the Name of Judith Anderson. You could tell that she was an aging very quickly as was all of the Indian women, who had to live out in the sun most of their lives, they let their husbands go out and find what they could eat in the meat line. There was still rabbits and squirrels that was in the woods so they spent their time there.

Judith was already busy doing things aro0und the tepee, inside and out. The men very seldom touched anything that pertain to women work for fear others would see him doing it. But William Anderson was a little different than the other Indians, that he was a half breed. A few years ago he came to this part of the state looking for beaver to trap and was captured by the Hopi tribe. Instead of killing him they decided to keep him alive so if they had to bargain with the soldiers at the fort, they could ask for food for him.

They kept him penned up for the time he was there and told him if he tried to escape they would kill him so he stayed pretty close to his prison. He had to be fed day after day and Judith whose name for the tribe was kicking bird was chosen to feed him every day. After about six months they got to noticing how each other looked at the other and they begin to have feelings for each other.

As time went on they began to talking more and more and the feeling between them became mutual. It got to the point that they would walk around the outside of the camp where hardly anybody would see them. One hot afternoon Judith decided to take him a drink and when she approached him he looked at her and asked her to marry him but she did not know what to say. She turns and ran to her tepee where he aged mother was she relates to her what William asked her. Her mother told her to sit down and she tried to explain that she would always be called a half breed's wife because he was white and she an Indian, that all their children would carry that with them as long as they lived.

If she wanted to live with that then she would give her consent for them to get married, but she would have to get the chief's ok also. Kicking bird went back and told William "But why do, I have to go to the chief, what has he got to do with it." He asked.

"He is the one that tell anybody whether they can come or go from the camp, he is the one that makes that decision." She said

"We'll let us wait until morning and them we will talk to the chief and then we will talk to your mother also if that will be ok with you. She shook her head as to say it was all right and then she headed to her tepee.

William sat around the compound where he was being thinking about the kind of life that he had lived up to this point and the kind of life he could have with kicking bird. He had been much of a wanderer all of his life. He had worked on ranches for a while until he could get enough money to go to the next town and get drunk or lose his money in a poker game. Then he got into trapping and selling the fur to fur traders and that seemed to him to be to his liking than working for a living. It always worked out good until he would get into trouble with the Indians and have to give up his furs to save his neck, but it has always worked out for him. Now he is thinking about settling down with a pretty young maiden that he loves and that he thinks that he will learn a lot from her and her ways.

Now he gets to thinking what is the chief going to say to him, being he is a half breed. What different does that make to him especially if he tells him that he will not take her away from the reservation. That they will continue to live there with the tribe. That he will fight with the tribe, but not against his own people. The only thing that he will ask the chief is that he wants to change her name to "Judith". This was his mother's name and she reminds him of her mother so much that he will ask the chief to let him call her by the name of Judith.

Sometime during the night he finally fell asleep and slept soundly until he was awaken by the dogs barking at a deer running through the camp. Then he thought that all the camp was awaken at the same time because all was looking out to see what was going on. I was not long after sunrise that kicking bird brought his food to him and she asked him,

"Well what kind of a decision did you make last night about talking to the chief and to my mother." She asked.

"I guess when you get ready I will be ready to go to him and see what he will say, then we will go to your mother and listen to her." He replied "did you happen to talk to your mother about this and see what her feelings about it was."

"Yes I did, but you will have to wait and talk to her yourself." She said "I will be back in about an hour to get with you and then we will go see the chief." Then she turns and goes back to her tepee to do her morning chores that she has to do every day.

In the last few months Williams beard had grown all over his face and he wanted to shave a little of it off but they did not allow him to have a knife so he had to just go and looked like he was. When kicking bird came to him he tried to explain that he needed a knife to shave part of his whiskers off so he would not look so bad. But she got him by the hand and led him to the chief's tent. She told him what to speak in the Hopi tongue to call the chief to the outside of the tent. He tried to talk to the Chief but he knew that he did not understand his tongue, so kicking bird was the interpreter for the two of them as they talked.

The chief tried to explain to kicking bird how their life would be outside of the Indian camp. What they would be called, how their children would be treated, but he said if you still wanted to go through with it, he would call a council meeting with the tribe late that afternoon and they would give an answer to their question. William was not expecting all of this time just to get married, he thought he would just ask her and that would be it. Now there was going to be another day's wait for the question to be answered. So now they went to Kicking bird's tent to talk with her mother.

Her mother was aging to the point that she wanted someone to look after her daughter because she knew that she was not long upon this earth, so if he wanted to look after her she would give her consent. Then she tried to tell them what the chief had told them how their life would be living together, even on the reservation they would be called half breeds. William told her that she would be taken care of where ever they lived. She would not have to worry about her daughter, or for that matter have to worry about herself. But now it was going to have to be up to the counsel to make the decision.

The day was very long for the two. William went for a ride across the reservation to the foothills looking for game that might be there. He was not only going to have to look for fur now but for the meat to put on the table. He was going to have to feed three now instead of one. He was hoping that would be the case after the council's decision. He rode until he thought the sun would be very low when he got back to camp. When he arrived back there was kicking bird waiting on him to go to the council meeting.

He asked her to wait a minute while he went in the tepee and got a knife and cut part of his whiskers off his face and made his self-look half way presentable to the men of the council. When kicking bird saw him she was surprised to see the difference that the hair made on his face and the way that it looked now. So now they are off to the council meeting and hoping for the best.

There was about fifteen old men and about the same number of the young men. They ask William and kicking bird to stand before and present their case to them about wanted to be married and for him to change her name. As William spoke she interpreted for the two. Then at the end he told them he wanted to change her name, and the reason why. They sat in silence for a few minutes looking at each other and then then chief stood and spoke to the men and asked if anyone had any ob. ejections for them to be married and what would be the cost for letting kicking bird get married. When they were in agreement the chief ask William to stand and listen to what the council had to say. Kicking bird was standing along his side to talk for them. Told him he could marry her for four horses, and that he had two moons to bring them to the tribe then and only then they could be married.

As they were leaving the council meeting he looked at kicking bird and says, "man are we ever going to get married, what else am I going to have to do to get you."

"When you bring the horses to them we will be married, and not until then.' 'She said

"Where am I going to find four horses that do not have a brand on them, because I know they would not accept them" he said.

"Let us go and talk to mom about it she probably knows where there might be some horses at for you to get." When they arrived at the tepee with her mother they told what he had to do and she told him to go to the mountains to the east and there he would find horses. He needed to take an ax and some rope to bring them home and an ax to fix a place to hold them in while he had all four of them. She told him they used to capture them all the time in that part of the valley. He bent over and gave her a kiss on the forehead and then gave kicking bird one and turn and as he was going out of the tent. "I will see you when I get my horses and I hope I do not run out of time" he say's

Kicking bird goes outside of the tent with him and watches him leave with a few tears in her eyes. She was showing her feelings for him already. All she could do was wave at him in the distance, then turn and start doing her chores for the day. The days seemed long for her as she done what she was supposed to do and then take care of her mother also. Her aged mother was beginning to weaken day by day as she watched her. She would cook good meals for her but she could not gain her strength that she had only a short time ago.

It was only about a week after William left that kicking bird's mother became gravely sick. She called in the tribe doctor, but he said he could not do nothing for her she was to week. Then she went to the chief and ask if they could get a doctor from the fort and let him look at her, maybe his medicine would be a little bit stronger. He told him it would be later that evening, but he would come out.

Later that afternoon the doctor came to the camp and was guided to Kicking Bird tent to see if he could her mother. When he examined her he told them that she was so weak that he did not believe that any medicine would do her any good. The best thing was to let her rest and give her plenty of fluid. He told the chief that he thought that she may have got some contaminated water from somewhere, that they all should boil all their water before drinking it, especially where animals would be walking in the water.

Kicking bird sat up with her mother, holding her hand until late in the night, then her mother just quit breathing and lay there very still. She knew that it was her last breath. So the next morning she sent for the chief and told him that she had died during the night and now they could take her to their burial ground They had special people that would wrap them in their burial clothes and put certain spices on them before they would take them away. Kicking bird followed along so she would know where they would lay her body so she could go back and put flowers on the grave later on.

Now she was by herself at night and she would cry the biggest part of the night then when morning came she would go about doing her jobs around the camp ground. Time was passing off so slow for William to come home, but she knew that he would be home with the horses if he went to where her mother had told him to go and do what she told him to do.

The first moon phase was already past and now they were on the second phase that the chief had given to find the horses. Every night she would stand and look out toward the east for a rider to be coming from that way, but so far she had seen nothing.

One evening the chief and some of his braves was walking through the camp and he came by her tent while she was working outside, "have you heard from William yet" he asked

"No not yet. Do you know how many days that he has left to be back? When is the next phase of the moon?" She wanted to know

"He has ten more days before his time runs out. If he is a good man he will be back on time." The chief replied.

"Maybe he needs a little more time. Maybe he did not know where there was any horses at and he had to go a long ways to find them" She said. Then the chief turns and walks with his braves without telling her that she would have some more time if he had not came back with the horses.

As the custom was Kicking bird had taken all of her mother things and put them in a fire and burned them so if there was any disease left on them it would be destroyed in the fire. If a tribe member was killed by someone they did not have to do this, only if they had a disease of some kind like her mother had. They could not determine her cause of death.

Late that afternoon while she was burning some of the things she sat down on a stump that had been made for a chair to sat on. While sitting there she fell asleep for a little while, and when she awoke from the sleep she noticed that in the far distance she thought that she saw something move. She kept her eyes glued to that spot for a long time, then all of a sudden whatever it was came up over a little hill and it was a rider with some horses behind him, she knew who it was, she knew it was William coming home to be married. She burst into tears as she stood there and watched him get closer and closer, until in a break neck speed she ran to meet him.

He jumped from his horse and they embraced each other for a long time and telling each other how long it had been since they had seen each other. He just walked beside his horse so he could hold on to her without letting her go. They both headed to the Chiefs tent to show him the horses and tell him that they were ready to be married. When William came up to the tent one of the braves ran into it and told the chief that William was there. He came out with a big grin on his face and said "I knew that you would be back, you are a good man William." Then he ordered the brave to take the horses and put them with the others in the horse pen. He then told William and Kicking bird that in the morning they would have a wedding celebration and that they would be married then.

"Kicking bird turns to William and says, ask the chief about changing my name. He turns to the chief and tells him that he wants to change Kicking bird name to Judith because that was his mother's name and he loved his mother and that he was going to love her also. The chief gave his approval and then she says, "let us go and I will fix you something to eat. Tomorrow is going to be a big day."

As they sat and talked and ate, William ask if she wanted to go somewhere special when they are married tomorrow just to be by their selves for a few days. They could ask someone to look after their tepee while they were gone. Kicking bird thought that it would be a great idea to take a few day and go somewhere by their own selves. She told William that she would pack some things to take along with them. Well I had better go to my place, the chief might frown on me being here tonight, so we will have to wait another day before we can sleep together. Then Williams goes to his tepee for the night and waits for tomorrow to come.

The next morning was bright and sunny when William got out of his tepee. He looked down at Judith's tepee and she was already working outside of her home. William took a brush that he groomed his horse with and went over his buckskin clothes that he always wore. Then he started down to the tepee of kicking bird to see if she was ready to go down to the chief's tepee to start the ceremony for the day. The tribes were already gathering along the path that the chief and the bride was to walk. The drummers was already out along the path way also getting everything tuned up... They lined up along the path from the chief's tepee to Kicking birds tepee where William would be standing.

When they arrived at his tepee he came out and told a brave to take William down at her tepee telling Judith to tell him to wait on them there. They would be there when it all got started. William thought, man another day to be shot, but he went down and sat in Judith's chair until he saw the chief come out of his tepee in all his fancy headdress and all the other colors on his wardrobe. He knew it was getting ready to start. The chief took Judith by the hand and started down the path to her tent as the drummers started their drumming. Before long they were standing in front of her tent with half of the camp around them. The chief took both of their wrist and tied them together and help them and said a few words over them and then put a little blood on each of their wrist and said a few more words when he then untied them and made a motion that they were man and wife. William could not but to help his self-turn to Judith and give her a kiss and all the camp let out a war cry for their happiness.

Then most of the camp came by and greeted them and wished them well. They told the people that they were going to be gone for a few day for them to watch after their belongings. William had already had their horses packed before the wedding so that they would just take off and get over to the mountains before dark. They were getting a good start on the days ride because the ceremony did not last as long as they thought it would. So they head toward the east to where William had found the horses at because he had seen some good hunting in the area and he wanted to go and check it out again, this time he would have all the time he wanted to take. As they kept riding away from the camp the sun was slowly beginning to set in the sky behind them when they found a good place to pitch their tent for the night and get settled in for the first time.

It was a good night for them both. Love had begun to settle in on them both. Then after William told her the kind of life that he had lived and now he wanted to settle and raiser their love making they began to just lay and talk about their families and where they had lived and settled. This continued on until up in the morning then they fell asleep. The next morning he was awaken by the smell of fried bacon and the smell of coffee that he had brought along. He rose and got dressed then went out to find that she already had breakfast ready to eat and everything made. He just thought to himself, what kind of woman that I have here.

While Judith was cleaning up, William went and got all the horses ready and then they both took down the tent that they slept in and put all their gear in it to hold it on the pack horse. He thought how wonderful that they could work as a team doing all of their work. William knew that they would be where they wanted to camp for the next few days by sun down so he just took his time as they rode and talked about what they were going to do while they were here. Judith told him she wanted to look for nut trees so she could have some to grind up for meal. He could not understand this because all that he ever saw was in a sack that was bought at the store. He knew that he was in for a learning experience. A couple of hours they were where he wanted to pitch his tent. Then they would go and look for animals and her trees.

When they had left camp, Judith had not even noticed that William had packed a rifle on both of the horses. While they were at camp she made mention to it and he told her that she was going to learn to use it in case she needed meat sometimes when he was gone. William turns to her and said "bring me the gun here and I will show you how to load it.' She did as he had asked her to do. He showed her the safety on the gun and told him it would not shoot if it was put on, it kept the gun for firing.

They walked over to a hill side and he knelt behind a rock and put his gun on the rock and took aim at the white object about fifty yards away and he told her to watch it, then he pulled the trigger and then it was gone. All she could say was 'wow'.

William says "now it is your turn, let me have your gun a moment. Look at the end of the barrel of the gun, then look mat the other end of the gun, you see that little notch there, and you put that notch with that rise on the other end and pull the trigger."

She takes the gun and lays it on the rock just like William did and looks down the gun barrel and he looks at her and says "wait a minute, you cannot hit anything if you have your eyes shut, close this eye and open this eye and pull the trigger." She did just like he told her to do and then she shot at the target and hit it dead center, to her and his amazement. They did this for a little longer then William said

"We had better go and see if we can find some animals to shoot before we run out of bullets, but first let me show you how to reload your gun. This is the first thing you always do when you get through shooting, remember this"

They knew that there was not going to be enough time to go today at look for animals so they just unpacked their pack horse and pitched their tent and cooked up a meal beside the stream that they had camped by.

After supper Judith said, "Boy it is peaceful and quiet out here. Where would the animals be from here?"

"They would be a little further in the valleys back in the hills, we will go in the morning and look for them and the nut trees will be in the large forest that you see over in that valley, again we will see tomorrow" William said. Then they settled in for another night of their life together

The next morning as he the morning before he awoke to smell of food cooking on an open fire and he knew that Judith was already up and cooking. So he get up and goes outside and gives Judith a kiss on the cheek and tells her he is going to get the horses ready while she finishes up cooking. He has just about everything ready when Judith yells that the food was ready come and get it. It just amazed William how well she had picked up the English language in just a few months that he taught her while they held him captive.

They sat and ate talking where they were going to ride and he told her that they would look for elk, deer and bear while they were riding so they could take it back to the tribe to be put up for winter. William already had the pack horse ready to go, then he loaded both of the other roses with a gun apiece. Judith looked at him and said today "Do you expect me to shoot a bear or a deer today."

"We are going to shoot whatever we see today, and I want you to shoot the first one." William said to her, "and you can do it"

They had rode for little over an hour when he spotted an elk and came to a stop with his horse and showed it to Judith. As they were trying to ride closer to it to get a good shot it spotted them and ran straight ahead of them as they watched to see where it went. William motioned that they would ride slowly ahead until they spotted it again then they would shoot it.

Again they had rode for about another hour when all of a sudden there ran the elk about a hundred yards in front of them like something was after it. William already had his gun out to try to get a shot when all of a sudden a shot rang out and Judith saw William falling off of his horses and he was shouting "Get off your horse, Hurry get off your horse and get your gun and get it ready to shoot. He no more than said this when all of a sudden there came an Indian from the bushes on his horse screaming and shooting at William just as if Judith did not even existed.

Judith knew that she had to do so0mething quickly, so she played herm gun upon her saddle and took aim at the Indian and pulled the trigger. His hands flew back over his head, his gun went flying and he goes over the back of the horse and lands on the back of his neck with a thud. By this time William had gotten to his feet and was still being his horse when another Indian came riding as fast as he could shooting wildly at everything without hitting anything, so William took carefully aim at him and hit him in the upper part of his chest and he fell from the saddle over to, the side of horse right on the top of his head. William knew that if the shot did not kill him the fall did.

Judith could see how William was bleeding and started over to him when he motioned for her to look at the other two Indians that were also coming toward them, but all of a sudden they turned and started riding away, but William took careful aim and let go with a shot and one of the Indians slumped toward the front of his horse as if he had been hit.

By this time Judith had made it over to William and saw how that he was bleeding in his shoulder that she made him get on his horse and they headed for camp. She told him she would come back later and get the other horses, but he told her to gather everything up now and he would help a little so they could take it with them, that he would be alright until they got to camp.

She went and got the two horses and he went and gathered up the guns the Indians had with them. All the time he was wondering where they might have gotten the guns at. All the time Judith was watching him to see if he might be bleeding more, but it looked like it was not getting worse. When they got back to camp Judith started to taking down their tent and putting their supplies in it to put on the pack horse when William said "what in the world are you doing"

"We are going back to camp where I can get a doctor to look at the shoulder and take that bullet out before it sits up some poison in it. You just sat back and let me do everything so you won't be bleeding too badly. We are going to just ride slowly till we get back home, so let us get started." Judith said

"If you start getting to weak to ride I will fix a sled to haul you on. So you let me know how you feel every now and then" she continued on. He spoke "I will be alright I think". It was not a very hot day, just the kind of weather that you would like to ride around hunting, but this was not that kind of day for William today. He knew that he had to get to the Doctor at the fort before he bled to death. He thought that Judith had done a good job of holding the bleeding back for the time being, but what will the riding do for it, he did not know.

Judith rode right alongside of him to make sure that things were going ok with him. They would talk and tell each other their feelings for each other, but now was not that time for that. She knew that they had to keep going to reach the fort by noon the next day.

Sometime during the night she got William off of his horse and feed him some food and they washed up to wake themselves up so they could keep riding for the night was going to be a long night. Hour by hour William could feel his self-getting weaker. He would reach down in his saddle bag every now and then and get some beef jerky that they had brought with them just to keep his strength up.

By sun up the next morning they could see smoke from their village but they knew it would be another three or four hour ride before they could see the people or the people see them. William was beginning to slump over toward the front of his horse. Judith knew that he was getting weaker but it was too short of time to give up now. She wished that there was some way for her to have them to go and get the doctor before they got there but she knew that it was impossible.

They were close enough now that some of the young braves had spotted them and came and see who it was. When they got to them she told them to take the horses that was tied to her horse and take them to the chief and let him see who they might belong to. The chief was ready to talk when they got there but Judith told him she had to get William to the doctor at the fort to get the bullet taken out of him, it had been in there too long.

The chief ordered two of his braves to ride along with Judith and William to the fort and that he would talk to them when the returned from the doctor. They headed right on to the ort which was only a two hour ride to it. One of the braves ran ahead and had the doctor ready to take the bullet out when they got there. All the time he was taking the bullet out Major sanders was there wanting to know how it all happened. They told him just the way that it happened and told him the bodies were still there if he wanted to send out men to pick them up if the Indians had not returned to get them.

He told William that there had been some Indians from some tribe in that area that was rustling cows from a rancher. The rancher had come to the fort to report it and that you two might have found them and they thought that you were there to get them for taking the beef from the ranch.

"All I know was that we were there hunting for meat for the winter and they attacked us before we had a chance to see what they were doing." William said

"I will send a man back to your village and let him listen to the chief and see who he might think that these Indians are. I have no idea myself. Said the major "I will make a report on it so if the rancher comes in again I can let him know that some of his problem has been taken care of."

By this time the doctor had finished getting the bullet out of his shoulder and told him that he wanted him to stay in his tepee for at least two days and eat plenty of meat to get his strength back. And he looked at Judith and said "and I hope that you will make him stay there for at least that many days."

Judith replied, "I will do the best that I can,"

As William finished dressing major sanders turned to him and said, "by the way I heard through the grape vine that they had a white person held captive in the village but I did not ever go to see about it because I never did have a complaint on it so I did not go check on it, was that so."

"Well I heard the same thing, but I think they have let him go now and turned him over to house arrest for the time being." William had told the major about them being on their honeymoon when all this happened. He congratulated them then went out to his office. They headed back to the village to report to Chief Mattawa about what happened. As they rode back into the village the chief and his council was there waiting on them to tell what had happened. They told them that they told the Major at the fort what they were telling them also.

The chief spoke up after William had related all that had happened to them and told them that the Indians were from the Choctaw tribe, but they were almost four days ride from their village... The chief related that they must to have been on a hunting trip, but he could not answer why they attacked them like they did.

Then William told them what the Major at the fort had said about them rustling cattle from one of the ranchers and that we must to have run upon them and it scared them so they thought that they had better kill us before they was reported and got arrested.

"I guess that does answer a lot of questions then on why they attacked you. You had better go and get to rest like the doctor told you to do before the squaw gets mad at you." The chief said. So they headed for their tepee to get that rest.

The next couple of days were miserable for William just laying around the tepee not able to do anything, He was not used to doing things li9ke this, and he was one that was always on the move. The chief came over the second day and talked with him about taking a small hunting party back over there and try to kill some meat for the winter. William thought that would be a great idea. He did not think the other Indians would be back over there to get more cattle. They would be far from their reservation for them to keep coming there.

As the sun came up bright the next day. William could feel the heat coming through his tepee wall and he just had to get up and get out of the tent. When he exited the tent there was Judith standing waiting to give him a morning kiss and to welcome him for breakfast. She had made him a comfortable chair to sit in so he could enjoy his breakfast. Some of the young Indians would come by on their horses going to the woods behind the village and they would laugh at

William and the chair she had made for him. Judith would jester to them and run them off.

Later that day William walked down to the chief's tent and talked to him again about the hunt that he wanted to take the braves on, and how many that he wanted to take with him. The chief asked him "how many guns do you have now"

"Four" William replied "That's not counting my revolver. And I got some ammunition the other day when I was at the doctor at the fort. We should be alright on them. I need to know who is going so that I may take them somewhere and learn them to shoot the gun so they can hit something.

"That would be a good idea" the chief said. Then the chief named off four young men to go with William, then he brought them in and introduced them to him and he told them he would meet them at the edge of the woods behind the village in about an hour to take some target practice. They grinned at each other for none of them had ever fired a gun before.

Then William headed back to his tepee to get the guns ready and the bullets that they were to practice with. He told Judith what they were going to do and she asked him if he thought if that was a good idea to go back and hunt in that area and he told her that he did not think they would ever come back to that region again for quite some time. William got his gear ready and headed to meet the young braves to shoot a gun with the hope of bringing home meat for the winter.

A couple of the braves had shot a gun before at the fort when they had a day for the Indians to compete in a firing contest, but the other two had never held on to one. Now was going to be their chance when they reached the woods to see how well they could learn. William showed them how to make sure the safety was on when they were on their horse and not to never point the gun at one another. He went over this time and again until they were tired of hearing about it. William was very surprised to see the young men learn so quick on how to aim and shoot. He told them to try not to shoot at anything that was running, wait until it stopped running then shot it.

After about three hours of shooting they were ready to go the next morning. William told them to be ready to make a two or three day trip, so take what they needed for those days and make sure to take some warm clothes because the air began to have a bite to it. He told them what to pack on the two pack horses so that they could have room to bring the meat back with them on the pack horses.

The rest of the afternoon was spent at his tepee with Judith as they sat around talked about their life before they met each other. He told her about his family the best he could remember. He told her he had one sister and a mother that was at home when the Indians came and killed them both and burned the house down around them. She said, "Where were you when the Indian came and killed your family."

"I was down on the creek fishing for supper when I heard the yelling and screaming, I knew that there was nothing that I could do so I just stayed hid under the brush until they left from the ordeal. I went to the house and found my sister out in the yard with three arrows in her body. I could see my mother in the house with her body on fire, so when it was over I buried my sister and took off to my neighbor house that was about three miles away before it got dark on me and I ran upon the Indians again..."

"Did that make you hate Indians after this?" She asked

"Not to the point I wanted to go around and kill them all." He replied "I knew if I ever seen one doing harm to anyone I knew that I would kill him, but it would be no more than I would do to anybody else".

"How did you feel when this tribe captured you, what did you think" she asked

"Well, I thought that my life had come to an end. I did not know what they had in mind" he said

"I just hoped and prayed for the best, and that is what happened, I got the best." He said grinning at her. It went on like this all the way up till bed time.

The next morning he awoke to a good breakfast and ate till he was full then he got his riding clothes on and went outside to see where the young braves were. He knew that yellow knife got up early but he did not know about the other braves. When he open the tepee up there were the four braves sitting on their horses waiting on him to come out of his tent. He motioned to them that he would be only a moment and he would be ready to go. He goes back into his tent and gives Judith a good by kiss and a big hug, she told him to be careful and come back.

"I will see you in about three or four days if nothing happens" he said as he headed out the teepee. He had just climbed on his horse when Judith made her way out of the tepee and stood there with tears in her eyes and waved to him again "don't worry about anything, I will see you soon" he yelled

The only one of the braves that could speak a little English was yellow knife. He had been around the fort to learn just a little and tried to speak it every now and then when he was at the fort. So William knew that he was going to have a rough time trying to tell the boys what to do and where to shot the animals to kill them.

They rode all that day until the sun was about to go down and then they made camp for the night and ate their supper and turned in for another four or five hours ride tomorrow until they reached the stream that they were going to camp at. The ride to the stream seemed short for them as they made it around noon and got their camp all sit up, then again William went over their gun with them as he handed each one to keep for his own.

The young men were eager to get started hunting, so they went for a ride at the edge of the valley to see if they could see any animals moving. It was about an hour when William spotted the large elk that he thought he saw before but this time the elk did not see them first. Yellow knife and another one of the braves made his way carefully around in front of him so if the others missed him they would have a good shot at him.

They had just got settled in when they heard a shot and here come the elk running right at them, they both took aim and both fired at about the same time. This time the elk went to the ground. They both let out an Indian scream and William knew that they had gotten their first elk with a gun. When they came over to Yellow knife and the other brave they were grinning ear to ear and slapping each other on the back. They made a sling to carry the animal on the fit on the back of one of the pack horses and when they got to camp the cleaned and dressed the elk and washed it clean in the reek they were camping on.

That afternoon while William was cutting up the meat the boys asked William if they could ride a little ways up the valley and see if they could see anything deer or some other elks running in the valley. He gave them his ok, but told them to be back before dark, which yellow knife said they would.

They had been gone for little over and hour when he heard a shot in the far distance. He wondered what they had shot at. After about two hours, almost sun down them came in with a large mule deer. William told them that he had not seen one that big before. He was going to gut it and hang it in a tree and wait until in the morning to skin it and cut it up with one of their help.

William turned in early that night, but the braves wanted to stay up later so they stayed up until late in the night then went to bed. William woke them early in the morning and told them it was time to eat before they went out hunting again. He asked which one was going to stay and help him clean that morning and one of them motioned that he would stay and help him. Then William motioned for him to get some water to clean their knives with so they would cut better and not tear the meat.

Yellow Knife and the other braves had spotted a large deer just a few minutes out of camp and they were sitting very still to see which way it was going to go so they might have a good shot at it. Then all of a sudden they heard screaming and yelling then shots fired back at their camp. They took off as fast as they could go to see who or what was happening, when all of a sudden they spot four Choctaw braves coming right toward them when one of them fired at them, and they all took aim, killing three of them and the other one had a bow with him so he took off to the right to get away from their guns, but they all fired about the same time hitting him also and he fell to the ground.

They took off to camp again but all they could see was to men laying on the ground. One was the young brave and the other was William, laying in a pool of blood. They had hit him with two shots right in the chest killing him immediately. They just could not believe their eyes to what had just happened. It was as if the Choctaw's were waiting for the others to leave camp then they were going to come and kill them and get their guns, Whatever the situation they were all dead now and two of Yellow Knife's friends were also gone.

Yellow Knife told one of the braves to go gather up all the equipment that he could find and their horses and come back and help them pack so they could get ready to go back home. They made a sling to go behind one of the horses to put their bodies in and one to put their meat on then they started back home. The ride back home was a very sober one. Hardly a word was spoken they all were wondering who was going to tell Judith what had happened to William.

They rode till about midnight and then pitched one of their tents. Two of them slept while the other kept watch. Then he woke one of them and he slept for a while. Around sun up they decided to move on without any breakfast. Their minds were not on anything to eat at this time all they wanted to do was get home and report to the chief what had taken place.

That day about noon they could see the smoke coming from their village. As they drew closer to their camp their hearts were begin to grow heavy now for Judith. They hoped that maybe she would be out in the woods somewhere but she was not. She spotted them from a long distance and she knew that something had happened for she could see only see three riders instead of the five that had left a few days before. She wanted to go meet them but she just could not get the courage to go. She could see now that William was not on his horse. Now she starts walking slowly toward the young men to ask what had happened.

They stopped when she ran over to the horse carrying the bodies and she saw William laying there still in a pool of blood. She knew that he was dead. She said "when you report to the chief will you come and tell me what happened." Yellow knife said "I will be back as soon as I tell the chief"

Chief Mattawa was standing outside his tent when they stopped at Williams's tent, so he knew that something bad had happened. Yellow Knife had gotten off his horse to tell the chief what had taken place and told him it was the Choctaw Indians again and that they killed all four of them before they had gotten away. He told him that they were not hunting when they were attacked but they thought it best for them to come on home with the dead and report what had happened.

The chief told one of his braves that could speak a little English to go to the fort and bring Major sanders out to the camp and tell him what happened. Yellow Knife was stilling the chief what had happen when Judith had to come and knelt down by the sling that

William was on just to be by his side one more time. She did not know who she was going to turn to, to go to the forest and get the nuts that she made her meal and flower out of. She and her mother had been many times but now with him gone also, there was no one to turn to.

Young bucks mother who was about the same age that Judith was had noticed the things that Judith had gone through and that she kept William from being killed by marrying him, although she knew that she loved him by the way that she acted she also knew all the trouble that their children was going to have when they were growing up and to be called half breeds. But she did not realize the strong love the two had for each other.

But now she knew that Judith needed a friend, someone to help her through these trouble times. She knew it was hard for her to lose her mother only just last month and now to lose her new husband by the hand of savage Indians. So she goes over to Judith and says, "Judith my name is Alena, I am young bucks mother, he is one of the braves that came back with yellow knife from the hunt. Judith all I want is to be a friend to you. You are having so much trouble lately and I know that you need someone to talk to if you will only let me be a friend."

"I need someone to lean on today, I just do not know why all this is falling on me. He was such a wonderful man, we wanted to have a wonderful life together. I just knew something like this was going to happen to him, I just knew it."

"Let me walk you back to your tepee and let's sat and talk for a while. I think we both have somethings in common that we can share." As they walked back to the tepee of hers, Alena began to relate to her some of the things that had happen to her. She told Judith how that her husband was killed by some of the government troops when he was just there to support the Indian cause and that he did not even have a weapon on him, but he was killed anyway. Now their son, Young buck will always carry a grudge against the troops.

As they sat and talked outside of the tepee they saw the Calvary patrol with Major sanders in the lead as they came up to the chief's hut. They stood and talked for about thirty minutes and then left. When they were gone the chief motion for them to take the bodies and have they prepared for burial the next day. Then the chief came and talked to Judith about what major sanders had said.

The chief spoke, "tomorrow Major sanders and some of his troops will come and get yellow knife and the other braves and go back to where William and the brave was killed and see what they can come up with, and why they are attacking the people that come over on the government ground and kill them. They will be gone for about three weeks and try to find why they are leaving their reservation and coming over where they are at."

"Tomorrow Judith we will have the burial right after sun up. You will be left alone for a few days and if you need anything during that time please ask for help" the chief continued. The burial the next day was hard on Judith, she did not know what she was to do now without a mother and now a husband to help care for her. While she was at the funeral, Alena was right there beside her all the way to comfort her and to be with her. Her son young buck was also there and Alena introduced him to her. She had seen him riding around the camp at times but did not know who he was or what family he belong to.

The next few days Judith just kept to herself as was the custom when some friend or a family member passed away. She worked around the tepee and then she would ground some meal from the nuts that she and William had brought back when they went on their trip. Just after sun up the first day she was to stay around her tepee, she saw the patrol out by the edge of the forest waiting for yellow knife and the other braves to go on their patrol. By now she thought to herself that they should be to where they were attacked at.

As the patrol approached the spot where William was killed, Yellowknife held them up and told them that this was the pool of blood that he was laying in. Then he told them the way that they had come in shooting and yelling. The Major and his men got off their horses and scouted around a little bit and he sent two of them ahead to see if there was anything else out there and look for a place to make camp for the night.

The Major ask Yellow knife where were the bodies that they killed at. He told him they throwed them into the river to float away from this spot. Then he said there is one of them about three hundred yards up the valley laying on the ground. Some of the men had already spotted it. Then the Major told them to bury it to keep it from smelling up the area.

By this time the two scouts had returned and told them there was a good camping spot up the valley a little ways, so they mounted and went on into the valley to camp for the night. Two men was on patrol all night just in case there was trouble. The Major still could not figure why there was Choctaw Indians in this part of the country, when they were supposed to be about one hundred miles to the east.

The next morning after all had ate, the major told them they would keep riding up the valley to the east for the rest of the day, and he sent the two scouts out again ahead of the patrol. That day they had traveled about fifteen miles to the east and decided to make camp. Again two men were put on night watch while the others slept.

Early the next morning they heard a shot off in the far distance it just was very faint but you could tell it was a shot. So the Major ordered about six men to head toward the east and check it out. The men headed toward the east as they were commanded to do. They had ridden fir about three hours when one of the scouts came back and told the Sargent that there was a body just ahead and he had not been killed very long they needed to come and check it out. It was a ranch hand that had come out to check on the fence and was ambushed along the trail.

The scout was sent ahead again to see if he could spot anyone and someone that had done this. He was gone for about an hour when the men heard shots fired and all kind of yelling going on, and then they spotted the scout riding his horse as fast as it could go and there was about six Choctaw Indians right behind him shooting wildly at him and they did not even see the troops who, when they got within rang open fire on the Indians killing all of them.

In the meanwhile the Major and his men had been moving toward the patrol all morning long and was in hearing distance of the shots that was taken place so they began a gallop to reach the men if they were in danger of some kind. When they arrived the Sargent told him about finding the ranch hand dead just a short distance back and he sent the scout ahead to see where the Indians were at when they attacked him and he just made it back to them before they got him.

Again the Major ordered a burial detail to bury the Indians and for two to go get the body of the ranch hand and they would figure out what to do with it. As they started to move out again "bring the ranch hand body with us we may run into someone that know who it is" the Major said so they started to move further to the east. It was still three or four hours before they were to camp for the night.

After about two hours into the patrol they saw some men riding toward them with the army's scout the Major halted the troops and told them to dismount and take a break. The scout brought the men up to the Major and told them who he was and they got off their horses and began to talk about some rustlers they had with their cattle. The Major took the foreman back to the body and asked if he knew him, and the foreman said he did that it was his hired hand, and he wanted to know where he got him. Then the major told about the Indians they killed, that they had a few head of cattle with them, then he told about the other times that they attacked people probably because they thought that they were being caught so they had to kill all of them.

The Major told the foreman that he would send a telegram to the Indians affair agent that was over the Choctaw tribe and see if he could keep them on their reservation in that district. That was what the foreman wanted to hear. The Major ordered his men to set up camp there and they would spend the night there and then they would head back tomorrow.

"You and your men are welcome to stay and have some food with us if you want to" said the Major

"No thank you we have a few fences to mend to keep the cattle in before more gets out by themselves, or by someone." Said the foreman "I thank you for all the help, if you need us you give us a yell we will be there. The men got on their horses and the major thanked them and for them to be careful with the Indians.

The Major sent two men back to the fort for them to get a wire off to the Indian agent over the Choctaw tribe and tell them if they do not stay on the reservation that the army will have to take care of their affairs by force if need be. The two left and the men made camp for the night with their guards out on patrol.

Back in camp Judith had been seen around the camp talking to different women of the tribe. Almost every day Alena would drop by to say something to her just to see how she was getting along. She would ask Judith if she wanted to go to try to find some nuts before cold weather came. Finally one day Judith walked down to Alena tepee and asked if they could go tomorrow and get some nuts to grind up. As they sat and talked they was wondering which way they ought to go to find the nuts.

"Let us go to the south today along the woods by the river there. Would you care if I carried William's revolver with me, it is a lot easier to carry than his rifle." She asked

"No that would be just fine. If I could shoot one I would carry it with me also, but I might shoot myself. But you go right ahead and carry one because I will feel safer that way" she said

"I will see you in the morning then" she said as she went on back to her tepee to get things ready for their trip tomorrow.

The night passed off very quietly. Judith arose up very early to get her sacks and her gun and the bullets ready to take with them. She had not been feeling well the past few mornings and this was morning was no exception. She was feeling like she could lose all her food that she just ate. Each morning was getting a little than the morning before, but she thought that one day she would go and see the tribal doctor and maybe he could tell her what her problem might be. But today she thought she would not mention it to Alena because she would not want to go and her feeling bad, so she would go feeling this way.

Yellow knife came by about the time they were leaving so they told him where they were going in case they did not come back for him to come looking in that direction. They walked along the edge of the forest that ran south along the river in the woods. They were told by the government that their boundary was on this side of the river so they stayed on this side.

They had walked about an hour then headed into the woods and they found a good number of nut trees like they were looking for. After about an hour or two they had about all that they could carry home this time. Judith made the remark that the next time they would bring the horse to carry them on that way they would have enough for the winter months.

On the way back Alena spoke and said "I noticed that a few times this morning that you were heaving like you were going to vomit or something."

"Well each morning for the last week I have been getting a little sick in the morning after I get up and fix my food, I try to lose it. I thought that I would go see the tribal doctor before long to see what it might be" Judith said

"Well I can save you a trip to see him, but you probably would not believe me, but you are going to have a papouse, you know a baby. That is what you call the morning sickness. It will go away in a few weeks. Some people had it bad others have it and not think nothing about it. You will just have to let it run its course. Fix you some herbal drink and it will help, but it will not take it away" Alena said

Judith broke down into tears and as she was crying she said, "Here I am going to have a baby and William will not be here to enjoy it with me. He said that he always wanted a family and now he will not get to enjoy it." As Judith was drying the tears from her eyes she noticed in the distance that the troops that had been on patrol was coming back and going to the fort. The troopers went on to the fort with Major sanders and Yellow knife along with three troopers came over and reported to the chief and told them he hoped that the situation with the Choctaw was taken care of. He related to him what had taken place while they were on patrol and that he wired the agent in charge of them to keep them on their reservation or they would face the military the next time. But the chief put out a warning for all to stay away from that part of the reservation until it was safe to go there.

As they watched the ducks fly south they knew that it was going to turn winter before long, so Judith and Alena went and picked up nuts from the forest one more time, this time they took the horse to carry them on so they would not have to go back till the spring had sit in. It was not long till the winter had sit in with a vengeance on the people. The wind howled through the trees and through their tents. Some had not prepared themselves for this kind of winter and they froze to death. Judith would catch a day that was not so bitter cold and she would go into the forest and gather all the wood that her horse could carry on his sling. Even then that would not last long as cold as it was. And all along she was getting bigger and bigger with the baby, but she managed somehow with it.

A couple of months had passed and she had not seen Alena for a while and she was wondering what was going on with her because she had not seen her. One morning when the day was going to be sunny and warm she heard someone calling her name from outside of her tent. When she went to see who it was, there stood Yellow Knife and he came to tell her that Alena was very sick and she was asking to see Judith. You must come to see her before long. By the way Yellow knife was talking she knew that she had to go right now and see her. So she told Yellow knife that she would be right there.

When she reached the tent she saw the medicine man there and she asked him what was wrong with her and he said that he did not know but it seemed that she had ate or drank something that was poisoned or contaminated some way or another. Judith asked if she could send Yellow knife to the fort and get the doctor there to come and look at her. The tribal doctor said he would welcome him.

Judith went outside and asked Yellow knife if he would go to the fort and bring the doctor to look at Alena because she was dying. So he took off in a hurry and was back in little over an hour with the doctor, but after examining her he said the same thing the tribal doctor had said.

"She probably did not boil her water and the water that she drank made her very sick. You people have been warned how to do your water, and what to look at your meat and see if it is bad or not. And if you do not do this this is what will happened" The doctor told them as he walked out the tepee and said a few words to the tribal doctor before he left.

Judith told the men that was there that she would spend the night here with Alena and take care of her through the night. During the night she heard her make a soft sound in her voice and she got up to see what she wanted but it was the last breath that Alena would make that night. So went and told the people that was to take care of people that die. Then she went to her tepee and wept most of the night. Now she had lost another of her friend who had befriended when she needed help, now all that is left of the family is yellow knife. He would have to look after his own self.

The only friend that she had left was Lady Bear that had been setting up with Alena also. They were very close to each other. Lady bear had a son that was named Young buck and she had a daughter by the name of Morning Dove who was very small. She only had seen her running around camp with some of the other children but had not talked to her. She did not know who she belong to until her and lady Bear was talking when they were sitting up with Alena.

The women also talked about the building that was going up just outside of their camp down the road a little ways. When they inquired with Yellow Knife about it he told them because they could not leave their reservation and buy their food or trade for food that the government would set someone up in the building to give the food out each month to the Indians. It would be just enough for them to get by till the next month.

They thought that would be a wonderful idea that way they would not have to go and gather nuts so man y times a year. It was not long before Major sanders came out to the tribe and explained to them how it would work. He told them one man would be set up at the store and he would live there and give the food to certain ones on a certain day all through the month till all had their portion of food given to them, and they would not all be lined up at one time. They all were to go down and sign up and let the man know how many they were going to feed in their tepee.

Things went pretty well for the next few months with the Indians and the one they called trader Joe at the food bank. Then for some reason some of the people's food come up short and he would tell them that their ration had not come in so they would have to wait till next month to get their supplies. Most of them had run out because they were not prepared to do without for that month and not have nothing coming to eat.

They would complain to the Major at the fort and he would send men out to check and he would tell them the same thing, but the truth was that he would sell their supplies to cowboys that was drifting from one place to another and then he would pocket the money and let the Indians go hungry.

Lady bear had started to taking care of Judith for her time to have the baby was very close at hand and she needed all the nutrition she could get to have a healthy baby. She could not go and pick the nuts she needed to grind to have a good meal all the time and Lady Bear was not going to go along, but they knew that the winter months was coming upon them before long and they would need them if the man at the store would not give them their ration of food.

They decided to find someone to take care of the baby and Morning Dove so that they could go and take a horse and get some nuts for meal that they could use in the winter. Then what they got from trader Joe would help them to have enough. One of the chief's wife's said she would take care of the children and they would not have to worry about them. So the next morning they decided to take a trip to the woods.

Judith told Lady Bear that she was taking the gun just in case they ran upon a deer or some other kind of meat. They were to go north east behind the fort for about a three hour walk to look for enough nuts that they would not have to make another trip in the winter months. They walked and walked to find the right spot and when they found where they wanted to stop, there were nut trees abounding. So they slowly begin to pick up and had not paid no attention what was the noise coming from that they finally heard. They left their picking up chores and went to see what was making a bellowing noise that was coming from down a fence line. When they got to where the noise was coming from, there was a black steer about four hundred pounds that had got its neck in the fence and had wrapped the barb wire around his neck and it was choking himself to death.

Judith had got down and grabbed the wire to try to pry it from the calf's neck and Lady Bear was on the other side trying to do the same but to no avail. They were afraid to try to unwrap the wire for fear of choking it more. They did not know what to do. The only problem was, they had not paid much attention of the time it was and the cowboy that had come riding up behind on the creek bank and sat and watched them for a little while before he spoke to them.

"Ladies it seems that you have a problem with a calf hung in the fence, may I help you" he asked

"This is not our calf, I guess it belongs to the people on the other side of the fence. We are picking up nuts and heard it crying to get loose but we have found out that we cannot help it. We were afraid that it was going to die so we tried to help it but we can't get it out. Judith said

We'll let us see what we can do to help you ladies as he reached into his saddle bags and pulled out a pair of wire cutters, and with one snip the calf was free, but it was so weak that it would not go nowhere but just lay where it was freed from. Judith said "I don't think it is going to go anywhere. It must to have been here to long and has lost his breath to long"

"It looks like the only thing to do is to shoot it and let the wolves have it to eat." The cowboy says

"But we just can't shoot it and let it lay here can we." Judith asked

41

"What else can be done with it, I can't take it home with me. It will not live long enough to get it back to the heard, so what else can we do with it." He remarked

"There are Indians starving to death because someone is holding back their rations at the food bank and will not let them have enough to eat, they can use it, not the wolves or wild animals, people needs it sir" Judith said again

"Well it is on your side of the fence so go and get your horse and we will drag it to that tree and hang it up and skin it and you can take the meat home with you how will that be.' He asked

"That would be wonderful sir. My name is Judith, and this is Lady Bear we have come out here to pick up these nuts you see under these trees and we grind them up and make our flour and our meal with them. We hope this won't get you into any trouble." Judith said

"No ma'am you will not get me into any trouble. I am foreman for the bar L ranch that cover this side of the county. We have had trouble with Indians carrying off beef from our range so they sent me out to ride and see how many they may have gotten away with, so this one more will not make a difference. It would probably die anyway before it reached the heard. By the way my name is Willie green. Everybody that knows me calls me willie." He said "I don't believe we are going to get this skinned today before night time catches up with us, you may have to make a tent to sleep in, and I will use my bunk roll here on the outside." He continued

Judith helped with all of the skinning she knew how to do and then packed all of the meat on the sling with the nuts. In the meanwhile lady bear went and set the tent up and before they knew it she had a good meal cooked with beef steak and all and they all sit down and had a good meal.

Willie and Judith sat out after they had everything done and talked for a long time. She told him about William and their marriage, and how it ended. And told her that her son was borne only a few months ago, and she named him Billie Anderson. She asked Willie if it would be all right if she changed his name to Willie Anderson. After talking for a long time they decided to go to sleep. She went in with Lady Bear and he laid on his bed roll under the stars. The next morning she and Willie was awaken to the smell of food cooking that Lady Bear had prepared for them. They finished eating and then wished each other well and they headed back to camp and he continued on his way looking for stray calves.

When they got back to camp they went to check on the children and they ran upon the chief and they had to tell him the whole detail of what had taken place and about the meat that the cowboy had given to them. The chief told them to keep it under their hat for fear that trader Joe would learn of it and cut their rations even more as he had been doing.

Judith and Lady Bear started to cook the meat before anybody knew anything about it and so that it would not spoil in the hot sun. After they had it cooked they put a layer of salt that they had gotten from trader Joe on it to help it to last longer. They knew if cold weather sat in before long they could keep the meat for most of the winter and it would last them that long if they took care of it. Judith was interested in the grease that she could cook out of it to make her nut meal stick together a lot better.

Trader Joe still was holding out their full rationed to them. Some of the braves got together and decided to go and talk to trader joe about short changing them on their rationed and threatened him with going to the Major at the fort about what he was doing, because one of the braves had seen him sell some of the supplies to a stranger who had come to the store wanting to buy some supplies till he got to where he was going. And he sold them to him. He knew that this was against the rules for him to sell the supplies. It was to be given out to the Indians only.

This winter on the Indians was a hard winter. They depended on the food from the government, but when it was held back they did not have enough to live on and some of the older ones died because of it. So the chief sent two of his braves to the fort and explain to the Major what was taking place. So the Major sends out two of his men to talk to trader joe and see if he would own up to the charges that the braves was telling him, but he held to his story that the Indians was given all that they were supposed to get. They went back and reported to the Major what he had said.

After the doctor was summoned to the village to treat some of the elderly people for starvation, when the doctor got back to the he goes to the major and tells him about the condition of the people at the fort and the way they were starving. This made his get to thinking about what the Indians had said and the reason they came to him so he called the Sargent to him and they talked about it for a while and he told the Sargent to pick somebody that that trader joe had never saw and bring him to the major and let us send him out to buy supplies and see if he will sell some to him.

So the Sargent went through out the camp and found one of the privates that had not been there long and took him to the Major and they sat down with him and told him what they wanted him to do. They would dress him up as a drifting cowboy that need some supplies to get him to the gold strike in Colorado that he had heard about and he needed some supplies. This was not to be breathed to no one in the fort or to the Indians. He was just passing through and he needed to know where to get some supplies and see if he would send him away without anything.

The Sargent had found him some old clothes that they had taken off of a body back in the summer and fix them up for him to put on and made him look like that he had been out traveling for months with all the dust they had put on the clothes. They gave him a horse without a brand on it, then told him to report to them the next morning or when he found out something out for them.

They instructed   him to ride to the west and come from that way like he was coming from Yuma he had been working at the federal prison there and got tired of it so wanted to go to Colorado and see about the gold strike that supposed to be there, besides that his sister lived close by out there somewhere and he thought he would look her up and say hello because he had not seen her in a number of years.

He thought to his self that he would have plenty of time to make up a story before he reached trader Joe's store. It was still three hours before sundown when he got to the store. They could see him coming for a mile away. They did not know who he was nor where he was coming from when he got there. He pulled his horse up to the hitching rail and went in and asked for something to drink if they had it. But trader Joe said they did not have liquor on the Indian reservation.

"Oh the stranger said, I did not know this was an Indian reservation. I guess I can get some water when I find it in the river somewhere. Look I have been traveling for couple of weeks and I need some supplies is there a place around here I can get some." The stranger asked

"You will probably have to go to the fort which is only a few miles on to the east and you will run right into it" trader Joe said as he looked around and saw the two Indians standing there turn and went out the door. Joe watched them as they starting walking toward the village. He asked the stranger if he still needed a drink and he said he did. When the stranger pulled out his cash Joe eyeballed it and said,

"You know I might have some supplies that you could use, how long of a trip will you be on." Joe asked the stranger

"Well I don't know, it will depend on how much I can put on my horse "the stranger said

"We will fix you right up in just a minute and you can be on your way" Joe said "which way will you be going from here"

"I will still be heading east from here I suppose that is the way to Colorado" the stranger said

"That's good you will miss the fort then" Said Joe

"I still can make a lot of miles before sundown if I keep on riding." Said the stranger as he handed him the money for the food. Then he bought his self another drink for the road he said. Then Joe wished him well and hoped that he would have a good future in Colorado.

Trader Joe watched him leave and watched him head toward the east and then went back into the store and started to counting his money he had just made on this sale. The soldier just went out of sight of the trading post and then heading straight for the fort. When he got there he went straight to the Sargent and showed him what he had got at the food bank, then the Sargent went to the major who old the Sargent to get about a half dozen men to go with them to the store and give trader Joe his walking papers. The Indians have been right all along and he could not see what he was doing to them.

They told the soldier to leave all the food on his horse just like he bought it and come along so trader Joe could see the evidence this time. The soldiers headed straight to the store and was there with still a little over an hour of sunlight left when they reigned up at the hitching rail. When they dismounted Joe saw the cowboy that had just left the store a few hours before and he knew that he had been set up and they knew the truth.

"Joe you have one hour to gather up your things and get out of here and if you ever show you face in this parts we will bring charges of murder against you. And it's a wonder if the Indians will just let you leave for the things that you have done to them" the major said. I am going to leave a couple of men her and you had better be gone in one hour or they will bring you to the compound at the fort to face charges that the Indians will bring against you."

"Get your horses and get your stuff on it and you get out of here now." The major continued and then turned to the two soldiers he was going to leave there and said, "If he is not gone in an hour, bring him to the fort". They nodded that they would

Then the Major turned and rode to the village and the chief came out to see him and he told him what they found out about Trader Joe. He told them that he was sorry about not believing them about him stealing from them. Major sanders told him that they would have a new man there by tomorrow morning and that they could trust him. And if they did not, they were to come and let him know about him also.

The Major gets on his horse and rides back by the two men that he left at the store and told them to stay there all night, or until somebody comes and relieves them tomorrow. He hoped to find a new man by then to run the store.

They were not paying any attention to Trader Joe but he was loading all he could get on his pack horse to haul away with him. In little over thirty minutes he was mounted and started to ride to the east of the village. The two soldiers decided to make them some coffee and make their selves comfortable, when some of the men of the village came to the store and the boys invited them for a cup of coffee.

Early the next morning the Major and a few men were there to take inventory of what was there to start with and they found out that there was more missing than they thought at first. While they were all working in the store a Yell came from outside

"Major you need to come here" one of the men yelled

The horse that trader Joe had left riding and his pack horse came back to the store. He told the scout that he had to try to follow where they may have come from. They had rode for a few miles when they found the body of trader Joe lying face down on the ground with three arrow holes in his back. He knew about who had done it, but he thought to himself, why raise a big fuss over something that was justified in the first place. That was his thinking.

"Major what you want to do with the body" they asked

"Bury it" he replied

"But Major don't you want" they started to ask

"You heard me, bury it" the major said then the major turns and rode back to the store with the new man to take care of it.

When the Major reached the store he asked one of his men to go get the chief and he would explain what was to take place that he would have to get new supplies to fill all of their orders, for them not to worry, they could have supplies from the fort to hold them over. The major asked the chief if there was anybody in the village that need some right now before their supplies had come in. The chief told him of two families that had need right now and the major ordered the men to load some of the food and take down there to the families today.

Judith and Lady Bear was getting low on everything but they knew that they could get by until they had more from the store. They had been helping a lot of people that did not have enough and it just about ran them out of meal and flour. Winter was just about to break again but Judith had decided to go and pick up a few nut for her and Lady Bear if she did not want to go. Just as she went out of her tepee there was morning dove standing there like she was waiting for her to come out.

"Good morning, morning dove what you are doing here." Judith asked

"I just came by to see what you are going to do today." She replied

"Well I thought with a pretty day as it is I thought I might go and pick up some nuts for me and your mother if she needed some, and she cannot go" Judith replied

"Well let's go and ask her if she can go," morning dove said "By the way do I have to call you Mrs. Anderson, or do I call you Judith, what I should call you.

"Well what do you want to call me? What would be good for you to call me?" She asked

"Well how about me calling you Ma'me, You know the white children call their parents of their mother 'grandma'. Well you are not my grandma, but the name MA 'me is not far from it and it would be all right for me if it is ok for you"

That is just fine with me but let's ask your mom about it if that is ok with her" Judith said as they reached Lady Bears tepee. After discussing the name, Judith told her that she was going to pick up some nuts so she could have some to hold her over for a while, did she want to go. But lady Bear told her that she did not want to go she was making some clothes for Young Buck, her nephew. Then morning dove spoke up,

"Mom can I go and help carry some of them back." She asked

"Lady Bear can you watch Willie for me for a little while. " Judith asked

"Sure I will." She said

"It is such a beautiful day today and I hate to let it go by and not go. Maybe by the time we run out again they will have the food store going again with a good person to run it." Judith said and then continued on as her and morning dive started out the door "I am not going to take my gun with me today because there should not be no rattlesnakes out today so don't worry about me shooting nobody."

Judith and morning dove went to the tepee and got them some canvas bags to carry the nuts back in. Judith had been to this part of the woods before and knew that it had some good nuts there. So her and morning dove struck out to go into the woods. They had been gone for about two hours when Judith remarked to morning dove that they had about all that they could carry back to the village. They had not paid any attention to the three Indians from the Okolona tribe.

When Judith spotted them they were just about to get into the water to cross the river. Judith jerked morning dove down behind the big log and told her to run as fast as she could and get young buck and tell him I have been taken by the Indians and I need help. She told her to run as fast as she could and not look back till she sees young buck or Yellow Knife and tell them what happened.

There was nothing that Judith could do but try to fight her way out of this but it did not work out that way. She glanced toward morning dove to see if she was near the edge of the woods. She could not see her now so she figured that she was not far from the edge of the woods. One of the Indians grabbed hold of her arms and tied them together and threw her on his horse in front of him. And they went back across the river with her in front of this one Indian.

They did not think that the other Indians would come across the river because it was forbidden for them to do so, and the sun was about to go down. The Indian that Judith was riding in front of every now and then would reach and grab her by the breast and let out a yell to the other two. He would speak something to them in his native but Judith could not understand all of it, but she knew that they were going to stop sooner or later and she did not know what was going to happen.

Meanwhile morning dove had seen young buck and came running toward him and the other young braves that had been out hunting. He leaped from his horse and morning dove was crying, "They have taken Ma'me, they have taken Ma'me' she said

"They have taken who, who are you talking about. Tell me again slowly so I can understand you. "Young buck told her

"There was some Indian in the woods where we were picking up some nut and they took Miss Judith with them and they went back across the river with her tied on the horse." Morning dove replied.

"She said to tell you to come and help her, Hurry young buck it is going to be dark before long." Morning dove said as the boys got to their horses and headed out to the river. They thought that if they could get to the river before dark they could see which way they were traveling. They already had their hunting equipment on because they had been on a hunting trip so they were already to go as they headed for the river.

As they reached the river, darkness had begun to set in on them. They were able to pick up their trail where they crossed the river because the grass still the water on it and their tracks were had some water in them. So they just headed in that direction hoping that the other Indians would follow a somewhat straight line so they would not be too far off. If it was the Okolona tribe they would be going in almost a straight line to their camp which was about thirty miles away, so they were hoping that they would spend the night somewhere.

Young Buck and the other braves had spread out just far enough so they could still see each other in the light of the stars. That way if they were waiting on them maybe at least, one of them had a chance to get away and go back home to tell the others. They had been traveling at a good rate of speed for it to be as dark as it was. They had been gone for about four hours when Young Buck motioned for them to reign up for a moment and then told the closest ones to come over for a moment.

Meanwhile Judith had told the boys she wanted to go to the bath room but they acted like they could not understand her so they kept on riding. The young brave that she was riding with would reach up and grab her by the breast, but the only thing she could do was to try to knock him off the horse with her body when he did such a thing. Finally the older of the boys told them that he did not think that there was nobody following them so they would make camp and let the younger one have his fun with the squaw. They pulled up in an opening to make camp, one he told to get wood for a fire and the young one to tie the squaw to a tree and he would take care of the horses. After about thirty minutes they decided to lay down and rest till morning then ride in to camp the next so everybody could see their captive woman.

The two older braves decided to go on to bed and let the younger have the first turn to try to rape Judith. She knew what was going to take place, she knew to, it was going to take more than this little one to get the job done. She placed her feet the way she wanted them because she knew what he was going and he went down on his knees and fell backwards on the ground in great pain.

As he was laying on the ground moaning in pain it woke up the other boys up and they s started to laughing at him and making fun of him.

Meanwhile, while all of this was going on, young buck and the other braves had caught a glimpse of their fore and had gotten close enough to walk to their camp because they were afraid their horses to try to do and the way he was going to do it. She also knew that it was not going to work that way. As the young brave moved toward her and stood between one of her legs, Just as he started to reach down to untie her waist strap, she raised her leg that was between her leg and it hit him right in the groin area would make a noise to their horses, so they decided to go on foot.

As the two boys got hold of Judith legs, one on each side they told the young brave to jump on, so he bent over and untied he waist strap that held up her clothes exposing herself to the other boys also, but just as the young brave dropped to his knees all he heard was the swishing of the arrow that hit him right where his heart was and he fell face forward on Judith and she wiggle to shake him off. The other boys reached to grab, their weapons when an arrow went into the chest of each one of them and they hit the ground also.

Young buck and the braves ran into the camp. And he told one to get their equipment and the other to round up their horses to take back with them. He asked Judith if this was all of them and she told them it was. So he laid her clothes back over her body and told her to put her clothes on while they got her a horse ready for her to travel on.

The trip back home was a little slower back than it was coming to get her. Judith cried about all the way back to their village because she was so proud of these boys she did not know how to thank them. They were taking their time to get through the trees that by the time they reached the river it was just light enough to see the river a little ways ahead of them. When they crossed the river there was bows and arrows everywhere pointed at them.

The chief had told them to go to the river and wait and see who was going to cross, Young buck or the other bunch for some kind of ransom. It was not light enough for them to tell who it was so they were ready for anybody, but when they saw it was Judith they knew it had to be young buck and the other braves, so all but a few went back into the camp with them while the other ones stayed on guard at the river crossing. As the boys reached the camp through the woods daylight was just about to sit in. Just about everybody in the camp was bout ready to get to moving around and get the day started.

They came to the chief's tent and told one of his braves to tell him Judith was here. He came out of his tent with a large smile on his face and wanted them to come in and tell him what had happened. He told Judith first what Morning dove had told them and he wanted to know if it matched with what she told them. But just as Judith got through telling him how the Indians came over and took her captive she told the chief.

"Look I have to go see if my baby is all right. Kicking bird has him.' Judith said as she ran out of the tepee

"Ok boys sat down and tell me all about what had taken place." The chief told them

They told about the time they left, about the time they caught up with them and what they were trying to do to her, but did not get the chance to do it. Young buck told how that they had killed them and got their equipment and their horses and brought them with us. The chief explained how proud of them he was for saving the ordeal that Judith was about to go through, but he told them it was going to bring consequences with it. The Okolona tribe would be here to take revenge on us killing three of their braves. Young buck spoke up, "but what was we to do with them, they were going to do harm to Judith one of our very own. We done what we thought we ought to do."

"You did just exactly what you should have done, what every decent American Indian would have done in your place. We will just wait and see what the consequences will be. But young buck you can speak a little English so you go to the fort today and tell the major what happened and ask him to bring some of his men and wait in the edge of the woods just to see what they plan on doing to us, maybe his being her will just put the fear in them. I figure that they will be here by about sun up tomorrow if he can be here then." So young buck headed for the fort as the chief had asked him to do.

So young went to the fort and approached the Major and told him what had taken place and about the kidnapping and the rescue and about the killing the three young braves to get Judith back and now the chief was worried that there would be trouble and he wanted him there to see if he could head it off. The chief also knew that they had him out numbered two to one when it comes to putting braves on the battle field. They were the smallest of the tribes from north to south or east to west. The Major told young buck to go back to the fort and tell the chief that they would be in the edge of the woods early morning tomorrow.

The chief called a council meeting that afternoon and put all the braves on high alert. That he wanted some down by the river to warn when they were coming so they could be ready. He also wanted some down by the river all night just in case they under estimated the Okolona tribe. They knew that they were fierce worriers in their day and time, and they probably have not changed. Any way they were all set and they went to bed as they did every night, but this time with their bows and arrows beside their beds

The next morning was a beautiful morning the air was a little crisp, the chief and his young braves was up a little before their usual time to get up. They were cooking when one of the braves down by the river came up to the chief's tent and told the braves that they were about an hour out, and do they need to do anything different. The chief told him to tell all but two to come on in and wait at the edge of the woods until they get there then come on into the camp. The chief already told them not to be the first to draw their bow, but let them do it first. The chief told them to tell the back two to come to the edge when they started to cross the river then come on in with the rest of the others.

The chief was sitting in the doorway of his tent when the braves started from the woods to the village so he knew that they were coming out of the woods in just a few minutes. He already put the men in their places with their guns and set some of them with their bows in their places just in case there was trouble. Now he walks out of his tent as if he was the greatest chief in the world. He walked a little ways out in front of his tent and just stood there and motioned for their chief to come on up on his horse if he wanted to

The chief first words were "I have come with a heavy heart this morning because three of my braves was killed by some of your braves."

"Is there any logic to what you are saying? So is it that you know who killed these braves and why was they killed if my braves did it?" Chief Katawas Said "you may be accusing my men of something that somebody else did. What reason did they have to do this?" The chief trying to get their chief to say because they kidnapped a woman but he would not admit to it. "You may be accusing my men of something that they did not do. Do you have a reason to blame them for doing something like this?"

"When my men found them dead hey tracked them up to the river but they did not see where they crossed it, but saw where there were four more that crossed later at the same spot, so why was your men on the other side of the river." The chief asked

"Do you have a witness that my men were on the other side of the river? If you do then they need to answer to me for lying if I ask them about it, and they will suffer the consequences for being there for they know that they have orders that they are for no reason to go across the river." Chief Katawas asked

"Do you have a witness that my men were on this side of the river? And if they were for what reason would they have been here on this side." The chief asked

"Well we might as well stop this bickering. so chief I just happen to have a witness that three of your braves were on this side of the river day before yesterday late in the afternoon. I do have that witness that you want to see." The chief said

"I would like see this sniffling snake of a brave that is hiding behind your back. I want to call him a liar to his face." The chief said

"Morning dove, there was a hesitation then" Morning dove come here' this is Chief Katawas. In just a moment here comes Morning Dove out of the tent next to the chiefs, then the chief spoke up and said" this is the young brave that was a witness to the kidnapping that took place the other day late in the afternoon, and if you want to see her I will also produce her,'"

"I do not think that you have anybody that is worth risking their life for to take them out of their camp, just to see what the boys risk their life for I would like to see her also" The chief said.

"She is standing right in front of my tent, you just look. Her name is Judith Anderson. "The chief said. "I think that we have gone with this far enough, DI will invite you down for a bite of breakfast if there is not anything further that you want to discuss, even if it is we can do it over breakfast. Because I am getting hungry." He said

"You know you may never get to eat another meal. I have enough braves to wipe you off the face of the earth and I might have to do that for killing my three braves." The Okolona chief said

"Even if you do want to start anything, you see that tree on my left, that gun is pointed right at you, just like that gun behind that tree on my right, then there is this gun behind my tepee pointed at you also. I don't know if you want to eat or to fight or go home but the decision is up to you." Pointed out Chief Kataawas

Then chief told him that the rule was that if a woman is kidnaped that person if caught is to be put to death. What does your rule says?

The Okolona chief spoke, "our rule is the same"

"Then why is this case different. My men saw your men trying to rape this innocent woman before they killed them, there is your witness." Chief Katawas The chief continues on, "did you know the white man has the same rule. They put the man to death also".

"It would be good to ask one if we could but there is not one in a hundred miles of here" the chief remarked

Katawas raised his hand and some of the men of Major Sanders came out of the edge of the woods, and Major Woods spoke "yes this rule has applied from the beginning of time and it will go to the end of time. It applies to me to you to this tribe here and to everyone, and we will enforce it if we have to be the one wiping those off the face of the earth. Just remember this".

"My invite still stands for you and your men for breakfast if you want to stay." The chief said. But the tribe turned and he motioned for them to head back through the woods And Head home, never to be heard of again.

The chief and the major sat and talked for a little while and then the Major returned to the fort. The chief had thanked the major for coming to help him in this time of crisis. The chief sat down in his chair in front of his tepee. The sun was shining bright now and the earth had warmed up. It seem like it was going to be a beautiful day. Then Judith and Willie came by going to their own tepee, when she stopped and said,

"Chief I do not know how to thank those braves for coming to rescue me the other night. That was going to be an ordeal for me if they had not gotten there when they did. Maybe one day I can prepare a meal for them all and invite them to my tepee to eat it." She said

"I may have to come to and make a speech for them" He replied

"You just want to come so you can eat, that's what you want." She said in return as she turned and walked away she said "we will see, we will see"

For the next few months things went peaceful through the village. The people that had been taking care of the store in place of trader Joe had been doing a wonderful job. They had even put out some garden seed for the natives to plant just to help with the things that they were getting from the government. Judith had planted some of it and had raised some leafy vegetables that helped with the meat that was given to her from the store.

Things began to bother her with the raising of Willie now by herself. She wanted him to have some kind of an education, although he liked a year or two before he was old enough to go to school somewhere, she was hoping at the fort. She needed to talk to the major and see if it would be possible for him to go to the school at the fort. She planned one day to go talk to the chief and see what he thought about sending Willie to the school at the fort.

It was not long that she was outside tending to some of her plants that she saw the chief outside of his tepee so she headed down to his place and ask him for a pow wow which he said he had a little time. As Judith laid out her plan for Willie to go school at the fort the chief listen carefully as she said that she would like to move her tepee down by the fort so he could be very close to the school if he could go there.

The chief spoke and said "you need to go talk to Major sanders to see if it would be possible for him to go there, then you need to think about the boys that will be calling him names every day in school."

"I will leave that up to him, how he wants to handle it." She replied

In a few days she had the time to go talk to the major of the fort about Willie going to school in the fort. And what he thought of it, if it was a good idea or should she drop it and just let it go by and have a child without any education. So she saddled her horse and told Willie they were going to the fort to talk to the major about his schooling at the fort.

Willie's hair was not much longer than the boys that went to school. The biggest thing was that his hair was cold black where the others were red to light headed. When she arrived at the fort she told the guards at the gate that she wanted to see the major and talk with him. One of the men politely got down from his post and told her to follow him. On the way to the major the guard was talking to Willie about hunting and what he like to do when he was at home. He was very nice to them both, but when he got to the major he asked them to wait there and he would see if the major was in or not.

He came back out with the major and he asked her to come in and asked her what he could do for her.

She replied "well I want to know what would be the chances of Willie going to school at the fort here. Or maybe I should ask could he do it in the first place."

"Well there would be some trouble makers that would object to it but we would have to work through it and he would have to be ready for anything. I know that there would be some hot heads that would voice their opinion about him being a half breed as they would call him. He needs to be closer to the fort to where he could be getting acquainted with the boys already before he starts to school the first day. They would already know who he is and know what they can call him." The major said

"I had planned to move closer to the forts but I don't know what that would do to my government supplies that I get living on the reservation." She replied

"Well you have to live in your tepee while it is on the reservation, or the tepee has to be lived in for it to receive the food for that spot. " The major said

"So as long as there somebody living in the tepee they would get the food, and if that person would like to help an old widow squaw then there is nothing that can be done to them is there"? Judith asked

"Not as long as that tepee is being lived in." The major replied

"I think that can be taken care of and I think you very much>" Judith replied

So Judith and Willie went to the village and told the chief what the major had said, so now all, she had to do was talk Yellow Knife or Young buck into living in her tepee while she moved William Anderson's tent up by the fort before winter sit in. Judith at night would sat and talk to Willie about going to school with the children at the fort and he thought it was a great idea. She would tell him of the opportunities that an education would offer him even if he ever wanted to go into the army it would help him there too. Willie seemed thrilled about it all and then she told him what the other kids was going to say and what they would call him, so he needed to get acquainted with most of them that was already in school so they would know who he was and tell them that he was a full blooded American.

So Judith went and told Yellow knife what her plans were, but she would still draw some food fro0m the government at that same address, because the other would be off of the reservation and she could not draw no food if she lived there, but Yellow knife told her that he would bring her supplies to where ever that she lived. He thought it would be a wonderful idea for an Indian boy to get an education and learn to be something. So every day she would take a little bit to the fort where she would be living until he gets him an education or maybe until he gets so far along that he might quit going all together.

When she got Willie in school she went and talked to the teacher and told her about his situation and the teacher reminded her that she already had a couple Indians in the school already and that she handled the situation very well she thought. Things went very well and then one day here comes Willie home with one of the biggest black eyes that a person ever saw and his mother asked him about it, and he said he and another boy had an argument and this was the way they settled it so now everything was just fine. She thought to herself that from now on she would let Willie handle all that he could take care of and she would handle what she needed to take care of.

Throughout the years while he was in school things seemed to settle down, and almost every day and on the week end he would always be hanging out at the fort with some of Major sanders men at the corral or some other place and just listening to the talk about bad the situation was in the united states where people were starving to death because there was no work and there was no food for them to eat. He would listen to them and come home and tell his mom the things that they were saying and she began to talking to some of the women about the situation and see if they have heard anything like this, and some of them had but they did not know what to do.

Late one afternoon Young Buck came to their tent and ask for Judith and told her that Lady Bear was terribly sick, that he had been sent for the doctor here at the fort to come and see what he could do. The tribal doctor had given up on her, so Judith told him to tell the doctor to come by and pick her up and find Willie so she could tell him where I will be at.

When she got there with the doctor she found Morning Dove there with her mother and a couple of women trying to comfort her all that they could. She was in terrible pain. Morning Dove explained to Judith what had happen after they ate supper, that she came down with terrible pain in the stomach area and the doctor said that she got hold of some bad meat or something. The doctor had warned them all about the poison that could come from their water a d their meat because it could not be kept cool in the summer time and that fungus could start growing in it and kill a person, and he continued to tell them this is what it seemed that Lady Bear had got hold of.

All you can do now is to try to make her as comfortable as possible and I will try to give her something that maybe will flush her body out, but it may be too late to do any good.

"Doctor you just go back into the fort and I am going to stay with Lady Bear tonight. I will send Young Buck to the fort to stay with Willie if he don't care to do this for me." Judith said

"Well if he don't stay I will find someone to take care of him tonight before I turn in for the night. You don't worry about him he will be taken care of" the doctor replied.

During the night the medicine that the doctor gave Lady Bear was flushing her out all right but she was too weak to go to the potty and they just had to clean it up the best that they could till it ran its course. But early in the morning while Morning Dove was fast asleep, her mother left this world, so Judith went in and woke her from her sleep and told her what had happened and they had about everything cleaned up and the tribal men had come and taken her mother to get her ready for her burial in the morning.

"Ma'me what am I going to do now that I am all along." She asked Judith

"Well why don't you come and move in with me at the fort and we will work it out when the time comes for us to do something." She said

"Do you think that the chief will care?" She asked

"Let us go to him the first thing this morning when it gets daylight, but now let us both get some sleep before morning gets here" Judith told her

The next morning they went to see the chief about Morning Dove going to live with Judith at the fort. They entered into the chief's tepee and Judith told the chief about Lady Bear dying during the night, and then she continued on as she told how that Morning dove was all alone, all her family was gone. Alena, who died back in the winter before Judith thought about moving to the fort., this was the only kin that Morning Dove had and she was her aunt. The chief sat very quietly for a few moments and then he said,

"Judith I hope that you know what you are doing trying to raise another one with Willie. The white man tells the world how much trouble is in the world and that the only answer to the problem is for someone to go to war so they may drag us all into that, but I hope not. I just want you to think what you are doing and as far as I am concern it is up to you and her." The chief said

Hearing this Morning Dove spoke and told Judith that she was ready to go home after the funeral. They had lady bear all dressed up in her buck skin suit with all colorful braids, and when Morning Dove saw her she just broke down and cried with Judith trying to comfort her. She was coming to the realization that she was now all alone in this world if anything happened to Judith and to Willie.

After the services for Lady Bear, the chief had one of his braves to get her horse so they could load all of Morning Doves clothes and her belongings that she wanted to take with her. And the two headed for the fort and Morning Dove had all her belonging with her to start a new life with her best friends.

Things went very well for the next few months while Willie was in school. There was days that he come home school with a black eye and he would tell his mom that it was taken care at school. She would ask if she needed to go to school and talk to the teacher but she again was told that it was taken care of at school. So Judith would let it go. Willie would get major sanders permission to go out on patrol with the unit when they were going only out for a day or two. The major would always make sure that Judith would know where he would be and what he would be doing when he was with the company of men that was under him.

On some of the summer afternoons Willie and Morning Dove would get their horses and go out for at least know which way to go and look for them. a ride in the country and they would tell Judith where they would be going so if anything would happen to them they would at least know which way that they went so the major and his men could.

Willie was in the eighth grade now and it would not be long for him to get his diploma from the school stating that he was graduated from the eighth grade at the Fort Stockton School. There had never been an Indian go that high in his school especially from this tribe of Indians. Most all the Indians were very proud of Willie and hoped that someday he could make a name for himself.

Willie would ask the major how could he enlist in the army and still stay close to his mom and his sister. Now he calls Morning Star his sister. The major told him that he would have to go off to some kind of training and that he would not be sent back to this post. It would be somewhere else. And also there was talk of war now that we had a new president. So there would be no telling what part of the country that he would be sent to. He asked the major how much money the soldier would start with in the army and the major told him it would be just under three hundred dollars a month.

Willie would go home and tell is mom what the major said and she would try to talk him out of going to the army but that was the thing that he wanted to do with his life. He tells his mother hat he hears about men out working digging ditches and other things like this to make a living for his family, but mom he would say, I can go into the army and you can have enough money to buy a house that they are talking about the government is building for people an just charging them only about twenty dollars a month. Mom you could have a house to live in and not sleep on the ground no more. Think about it mom.

"Mom it is something I want to do for you and Morning Dove. But you know I would not do it without your permission. I now I would be away from home for a long time but we could have what we have never had before. Mom you probably need to talk to major sanders and see what his opinion of me going to service means to my future" Willie told her

"ok let me talk to the major and see what he says about it and then we will talk some more.' Judith replied

"Ok mom" Willie said "I will wait and see what he has to say, but you need to consider the money that I will be making and the help it will give to you and to Morning Dove."

The more Judith thought about Willie wanting to go into the army the more she was scared but she wanted to talk to the major and see if he thought it was a good idea for him to be in the service and be away from home, so she decided to talk to the major, so she set up a time for the next day and she went to meet him.

"Hi major sanders, I think you know why I am here to talk to you about. It's Willie wanting to go into the military. It scares me to think about him being away from home and me never knowing where he may be at or what he is doing." She said

"You know Judith that is a very hard decision for a mother to make, but yet we are going to have to turn loose our children sometimes and use the resources that they have gained in this world. Like him going to school and getting that education so that he can use it somewhere and this is all that he has ever known is the military. I think he will make a great one." The major said. "Judith the world is changing and we cannot do nothing about it but go with it and change with it. The government wants to build these houses so that you may buy one to live in and this way you can let Willie pay for it with his military money."

"Just like today, we do not ride horses except for pleasure and we used to ride them because there was no other way for us to go. Look at the railroad just a few miles away so we can go across the United States and see all the country in a week or so, this is all changing and we do not want to be left behind." The major continued

"All I can tell you is that I do not know where he will be stationed at. I do not know where he will be taking his training at, but they will let him come home before he has to leave for a long time. Judith I do know that there is trouble in the world and there is going to be war but if there is war he will have to go anyway, so it will be better if he gets his training in before it happens." The major said

"If he does decide to go you both come over to me and we will decide which way will be best for you to get his money at home with you where you will have some to run the house with and we will sign the papers that way." The major replied.

"Give me a couple of days to be with willie and see what he really wants to do and we will get with you then " she said as she headed for the door and waved good bye to him. She went back to the tepee and pondered on the things that the major had told her. When she got back home she found willie and Morning Dove out with the horses riding back in the hills so she just sat and pondered on the things that could happen to him if he went in to the military, yet she also thought on the things that he could waste his life just hanging around at the fort and not do nothing.

When they returned home she had fixed a good meal for the two of them and sat down with them to eat their supper when Willie spoke first,

"Well what did the major say about me going into the military, mom? Did he think it was a good idea for me to go? Then again maybe I should ask you, what do you think of the idea? "Willie said

"Well son he thought with your education that you may be some kind of an officer or something like that. He also spoke out that there might be a war come along in a little while and that is the thing that bothers me son." She replied

"Mom even if war comes I will be one of the first ones to go and you and the major know that is the truth." He said

"Yes he said that. I guess my only concern is that you will be so far away from home, that is what bothers me." She said

"mom I guess that I just as well tell you now and for you to be told later, and that is I have asked Morning Dove to marry me when I get back home from the army, that way I will have enough income to make her and you a good living, and we can buy one of those houses that the government is going to build. Maybe you two can have it picked out when I get ready to get out "He said

"Well we will go over tomorrow and sign the papers and then the major will tell us when you and some of the other boys will be ready to be shipped out to your training area." She replied

After the night had passed and Judith did not get any sleep for thinking about what might happen to her son while he is in the army. They had a good breakfast and then they went to the major's office and to sign the papers. There was two other boys that was doing the same thing that Willie was doing and their mothers and their fathers was there with them. The mothers were crying and the fathers was giving them advice as to what to do and what not to do. Finally after all of them was signed in the major asked if all would be seated and he would go over their details the best that he could do. He knew that they would go on the train over to the county seat and be given some test and then sworn into the military. Then they would be let to come back home for a day to two to get things in order to leave for their training. And at that time they would be told where they would be taken their training.

The major told the boys to be there Monday morning and they would go to the county seat and

They would be given their physical and other test to determine what qualifications that they had then they would come home to be shipped out for training. And then and not before then would they be told at what part of the country they would be going to.

"Major I want all of my pay sent home. I just want enough to buy some snacks with" Willie said

"That will be for the pay master to decide when you get into the service." The major said.

The next couple of evenings the two were found out riding so that Willie could see the country side for maybe the last time. Judith was very proud of willie and Morning Dove going to get married when he get back out of the service. Now she knew that her boy would be taken care of after she was dead and gone.

Monday morning came around very fast and Willie decided to go to the major and ask him what time they would leave and he told them that they would leave at nine o'clock sharp out in front of his office. There would be a bus sitting there waiting on them for him to be on it. The three of them made their way to the major's office and the bus was already sitting there waiting for his pick up to get on board so he could head out.

Tears had already begun to come out of both of the women's eyes so willie had to turn away so he too would not be seen crying in front of the other boys and their mothers. Then the driver said to the boys "ok let us all get aboard so we can get there and get back before the sun goes down on us today and we cannot find our way back home". As he closed the door of the bus and Judith and Morning Dove found the window where Willie was sitting and waved and throwed kisses at him and he did the same back to them.

As the bus pulled out of the fort gate the two women looked at each other and both started to cry and to hug each other when the major walked up and said,

"Now ladies things are not that bad, he will be back before the day is gone. He is just going to register for the army and to take a few tests both physical and mental, so he will be back today, you just go on home and don't worry about anything." So the women went on back to their tepee talking about how Willie may feel about going off and leaving them all alone.

The day had passed off very fast. Judith had spent most of the day putting her food away that young buck had brought to her for her monthly supply. The talk around the fort that the government was going to discontinue to help the Indians. They were to get themselves a job at the army factories that they were going to build. Judith had already found out about the jobs that the government was going to offer to the people and she had already told the Major that she wanted to sign up to be one of the first in line for the jobs that they were offering.

So far the jobs were just in the air but they had already started to break ground for the new factory over at the county seat. That mean one thing to the military and that there was going to be war somewhere else besides the pacific. The tribe had already had some young men to go to the pacific to fight the Japanese. Some of them were already killed and brought back home for burial in their tribal way. Judith had taken all of this in and she did not want to do her son the same way.

The day had passed off so fast that they did not even notice that the bus had already arrived and they did not even see Willie coming out of the fort and coming toward their tent until morning dove ran

To meet him about half way and gave him a hello kiss on the cheek and he ask. "Where is mom at."?

"I think that she is in starting supper. I think I could smell it when I saw you coming. She will be glad to see you." morning Dove said

As they sat down to a good supper Willie told them the things that he had to go through. He told how hat some of them were good and others were bad, how that all the boys had to run around without any clothes on all day for their exams. He told Edith that they would be contacting Major sanders in the next day or two to tell him where they wanted us to go for our training.

Willie had spent most of the next couple of days going out to the village and talking to the chief. Chief Katawas was getting very old now and he already told them that Yellow Knife would be their next chief. That they were to respect him like they had done him all these years but now he knew that his days were already numbered and his time left on the earth was just so many days now. He told Willie he needed to get ready for more changes that was coming to the village and to the fort. The things that you see now will probably not be here when you get back. The people will be living in houses and we will be paying for them. We will be going the white man's way, but that is a good thing they have feed us for a number of years and now they want us to fight for them, but the good part of that they will pay us to do that, and they will build us those houses to live in. It will be good my son when you return. I will not be here but you will still have a leader when you get home, good luck my son. Then Willie turned and walked out of the Chief's tepee for the last time to ever see him. He died while Willie was in basic training. He goes Back to their tepee by the fort and finds his mother and Morning Dove looking at a folder they had picked up at the trading post and it was about the things that they could put in the homes like a stove to cook on, a couch to sit on, things that they had never seen before except in the fort where other people lived.

"What are you two doing, "willie asked

"We are just looking at pictures of those houses that they are building down by the fort entrance and they said they would be available in a month or two. So we thought that we would get our name in so we could be one of the first to get to live in one " Judith said and she continues on " Maybe by the time you come home the next time we will be living in one."

"That would be a wonderful thing if that would come true" Willie said. "Then maybe Morning dove and I can find us one of our own and we both can have one." 'Mom I did find out from the major that I will be leaving tomorrow morning again, this time for my basic training. And that I will be coming home after about six months away. It will only be for a short time then I will be gone for a long time and when I get home Morning Dove and I will be married and start a family of our own."

Son I hope all this works out for your good, and that you two can be married and have a grandchild for me to spoil." Judith laughed

Again the next morning the three of them walked over to the bus depot where he was to ride over to the county seat and catch the train for some part of southern California. Again there was two of the tribal boys going on the same bus, so this gave them something to talk to each other about. The two boys could only understand only a small part of the American English, but Willie learned the best part of his while he was in school and from his mother.

Again the women could not help but to cry when they saw Willie get on the bus to head off to where they knew not. Judith had never traveled more than ten miles out of the fort and morning dove had not gone that far. They had tried to keep up with everything that was happening around them by reading the newspaper that somebody had threw away.

Willie was already acquainted with how Sargent's acted when they have new recruits to put on the field of battle. He had been with new men that came to the fort and went through some training that he was going to go through. He knew it was going to be rough. He kept telling Lone wolf that they were going to stand in their face and shout at them just to see how much they could take without breaking and hitting them. They know if you can hold up to what they dish out then you will be a good soldier. In a few days they will see this.

It was in the afternoon when they arrived at the training station and the driver told them to wait for him to go and get them someone to guide them to their barracks. They needed to get off the bus and form a line so the Sargent could talk to them. As they got into a line, here come a man with a very deep voice and he stood and looked at them for a moment and in a sweet voice said, "Hello men" and the men spoke back "hello sir"

After that, it was the last word that they spoke all day without the Sargent being in their face and yelling at them. He then, after about an hour of hollering at the men he took them to their barracks and told them how he wanted it to look every day, how the bath rooms would look every day and if they did not look that way, then every man would go on a hike of about ten miles over all kind of terrain that they could walk over. So they had better be cleaned up.

"Oh by the way my name is Sargent Malone, I want you to remember that name. I want you to remember that name because if you ever want anything you are going to have to tell them Sargent Malone sent you to get it. Do you all understand."?

"Yes sir" was the answer from all the men at once."

The Sargent told them what time to go to the mess hall and after that they would have a little time to get their clothes in order and then tomorrow they would be give military clothes. And tomorrow would be the day that they would learn how to march. Then everything would go from there.

Willie had found out where the post office was so he could write to his mother and to Morning Dove. He would tell them everything that was taking place, and how the training was going. Then in about a week or two he would receive a letter back from his mother and Morning Dove would also write about what was going on at the fort. The only thing that they had not told him was that they had already got one of the government houses and was living in it. They were waiting on him to come back home to see it before they told him about it.

Things went well with Willie and lone wolf while they were at training. Willie, with his education they had gave a special class above some of the other men. It only says that he was in charge of certain items that some of them were not. It also carried along with it a little more pay for him to send home to his mother and for morning dove to save for their marriage when he comes home to stay.

Now with training over the boys were told they could go home for ten days and then they were going to Germany for the war that was being fought over there. They did not have time to write to their mother and tell them that they would be home this certain weekend but they came home and did not tell anybody about it till they were there. Willie did not know the house that Judith lived in so he went to the fort to see Major Sanders and ask him where his mother had moved to and he said,

"Go get in the jeep and I will show you where she lives now, they will be surprised to see you, you did not write and tell them you were coming." The major asked

"I did not have time to write and for her to get it before I came home, it all happened all of a sudden" Willie replied

"Some of the women got her and morning dove settled in and showed them how to work everything and they have been really excited about the house." The major said "Here we are son this is their home now just jump out and tell the major said hello."

Willie went to the door and knocked twice before morning dove came to the door and saw that it was Willie standing there with his duffel bag around his shoulder. Before she yelled for Judith she grabbed Willie around the neck and almost choked him to death and gave him a large kiss. And then she yelled,

"Ma'ma, Ma'me Willie is home. Ma'me come here quickly." Judith was in the kitchen cooking supper when she heard all the yelling and she came running and saw Willie and the tears came streaming from her cheeks,

"My boy, my boy it has been so long since I have seen you, you could have wrote me and let me know you were coming home." She said

"But mom they did not give me time for me to do that. I just had time to pack my bag and go catch the train to get here today. They only gave me ten days home leave before I have to be shipped out again." Willie said

"Mom when I go to Germany it will be for a long time they say. Then I will have time to write to you. But now I want morning dove to take me to the village in the morning so that I can visit with the chief and let him know what I have been doing." Willie replied

"But son you know that the chief Katawas is dead, he died right after you left and went to training and I guess I forgot to tell you in my letter. Yellow Knife is the new chief now, so you will have to go to see him instead." Judith told him "But anyway let me finish supper now and you can tell us all that has happened while you were away"

"I will go and help Ma'me while you put your stuff away in this bedroom here. It is mine while you are away."Morning Dove said "so I will bunk on the couch while you are here". Willie gathered up the bag with his clothes in and went to the room to take his clothes out while he was there on leave. After he had taken his clothes and hung them in the closet that she had made space for he backed up for a few moments and just looked at the room for some time, then morning dove yelled.

"Willie you need to come and wash up and let us eat before we all starve to death" Morning Dove yelled.

Willie came into the room and stood looking around and before he could say anything Judith spoke up and said "what are you looking for son.'"

"Well I am looking for the water to wash up with, where do it come from." He asked

"Son it comes from the old pump that sits on the sink over there. And it sure beats carrying it from the creek like we used to do when we were in those tepees in the village." Judith said then they sat down and enjoyed a quiet meal together and then went and sat while he told them all that had taken place while he was in training. The time passed off fast and it was almost midnight before they knew it, so they all turned in for the night.

During the week they would catch a bus and ride over to the county seat and look at clothes and things that they were going to buy when he comes home for good and they get married. Morning dove could not wait for that day they were married and then start a family. She knew Ma'me would enjoy some grand children before she got to old.

The factory that they were building outside of town would be hiring in a few months and Judith already had her application in so she would be one of the first to go to work. She did not want Willie to know that she was going to work at the factory, so she held back on telling him. She wanted the extra money for them two when he return home from the army. They were never expecting anything to happen to Willie while he was overseas fighting. They were planning on him just going over there for a year or two and then come home and get married and start a family. Sometimes things just do not happen the way you want them to.

So far the next ten days they would enjoy the company of each other and Willie and Morning Dove would go horseback riding out to the village and talk with the people in the village and enjoy the company of the people. Willie wanted to show off the uniform that the army was furnishing him to wear. He wanted the people to see it.

The days for him and Morning Dove passed off to fast and he had to load up on the bus again on Monday morning and go to the county seat and catch the train to Phoenix and then catch a plane to fly to New York and then on to Germany. Then he would be told what they would be doing and where they would be at in Germany.

Willie had not listen to the radio at any time he was home for he did not want to hear how many of our boys had been killed. He wanted to hear just good music and good news. Willie was experiencing things that he had never thought he would. The airplane ride from the United States to Germany was his first and he did not like it one bit, but he knew that was the way they had to go.

When they had reached their destination in Germany by airplane, Sargent Malone used a loud speaker to gather his men together and told them that they were going to convoy them to the front lines. That their trip would be riding for eight hours in the back of the truck, and then they would have about the same amount of walking to get to the front to relieve some of the men that had been fighting on the same line for months. Willie and their battalion was to be their relief.

All of the trucks were already lined up for them to get in. So the Sargent gave the instruction to load in the truck as many as could get in and they would head out, and try to get to their point of walking by day light. So it was not very long till the truck in the convoy began to roll and the men just leaned against each other to try to find a quick nap because they knew that when they got there it would be just out of the truck and then hit the road for the eight hour march.

The weather was beginning to turn cold and riding in the back of the truck did not help nothing to warm up. The only way they could get any heat was to lay close to each other. After about seven hours the light began to show in the east and it was getting daylight, yet all the men could see was out the back end of the truck, and that was not very far because a rain began to fall very lightly.

About an hour after sun up the convoy pulled into what the men referred to as a staging area, and from that point on they had to walk in the rain over muddy roads that has been wore out long before these boys got there. Some of the boys were always complaining about something, and the weather was the thing that was talked about now.

It had only been a little over forty eight hours away from sunny southern California to the worst kind of conditions that the men could experience, yet they knew that it had to be done. The men they were taken the place of had been here for the last six months walking in the mud every day, day after day and now it was going to be their turn.

When they had the time they would talk to the men in the other battalion and they found out that they had lost almost half of their men, either by infantry fire or by starvation. It seemed that the Germans could tell when they had a convoy of food coming in and they would shoot it up to where they could not use it for anything. The commanders said that they had the best decoders in the world, they could decode any message that they put out, and the Germans knew what they were talking about.

The men were close enough to hear the battle going on at times. Sometimes you would think it was not going to stop for any length of time, then all of a sudden it would let up for a little while before it would start again. Sargent Malone had got his men in order to march and he headed them to the front line. They would meet men coming from the front line and they looked like they were dead men. All they were doing was going back to the staging area and get a few rest and then head back to the front line again.

The men in Willie's company had never heard anything like this in their life. They thought that the training that they had gone through was rough, it was not going to be nothing like this. Sometimes the shelling would not stop for hours on hours. Some of the men would just about go berserk, or out of their mind. They would try to sleep but the noise was just too much for that. Every now and then there would be some men come firing at them across the field that was between them and they would return the fire and kill most of them before they would quit firing and return back to their side.

This went on for days and then one day Sargent Malone told the men they were to move up and try to take the town that they could see in the distance. He told them that they would have to fight their way to the town so watch where you are doing. There would be a few head up on the right and then a few on the left before the main column moved up the center. They had only gone a few hundred yards until out of nowhere, bullets started to flying out of the patch of woods that was straight in front of them. Two or three of the men were killed and a dozen were wounded and the bullets were still flying. Then the company on the left started to fire from their position, and the one's on the right open fire on them also, now Willie and that company could get a shot in every now and then and after a while they had captured about three hundred men from that patch of woods.

Sargent Malone had a few dozen men to take the prisoners back and find someone that was going to the staging area and let them take them back with them, if they made it back at all. He knew that this was war and he knew what they had done to some of our men when the captured them. So all he could do was turn them over to someone going to the higher ups. For hours the men had laid in the mud fighting these. Willie was like some of the other men they could not figure out why we were fighting these men when they looked just like we do. Some of them were even crying just like some of our men were, they just could not figure it all out.

All day they lay in the mud trying to gain a little ground, then all of a sudden there would come heavy artillery trying to hit them, and after that they would send in some more men to die or try to kill Willie and his boys.

Sargent Malone, when he got the chance he would tell the men to move forward, only to run into more Germans. Night time had fallen on the men and all you could hear every now and then was a single shot. Probably a soldier thin king that he saw something move. That went on all through the night. Sleep had not come to these boys now for a number of hours. Their thought was if they could get to the town ahead that maybe they could find some relief there and a place to fall asleep. Their only hope was that the Germans was left and gone.

The Sargent was on the radio the next morning and told the commanders that his men had to have some relief. They had not slept in the last three days, and they did not have a good meal since they got to Germany.

"We were hit again by their artillery when we tried to get another convoy of food through. They decoded our messages again. It is just like someone is telling them what we are saying right to their face" The radio man replied.

"If we don't have it we cannot send it to you" he said "You just hang on a while longer and maybe we can get something to you" the commander replied

"We will do the best we can, but I do not know for how long" the Sargent replied.

"Thanks" was the only answer on the other end of the radio

It was about an hour before day break and the Sargent told the men to pass it on, for all of them to start moving forward and if there is any shooting for them to hit the ground. He wanted to get to the town to see if they could air drop them some food and some ammunition to fight with. After about an hour of cautiously moving forward they were coming out of the edge of the woods.

Now they could see the edge of the town very clearly and it did not seemed to be nothing in their way, so they stepped it up a little more until they got within firing distance and a single shot rang out hitting one of the men between the Sargent and willie. He was dead when he hit the ground. This kind of shook up Willie for a moment. He Yelled,

"Sargent, what are we going to do?"

"You just stay down. Tell about six men on the right and on the left to take a run for the town and flush out the snipper that they have left behind and kill him. The men took off in a break neck speed and tried to get there before he opened fire again on the men. Then the Sarge told the men to watch and try to see where the German was firing from so they could radio the men and tell them. He fired twice at the men running hitting one of them in the leg, but the others made it to the town area. The Sargent got on the radio and told them where the shot came from, and you could see the men running to that area. The man looked out of the window where he had been shooting from and one of the Sargent's men shot him right in the face. Then the Sargent motioned for them to move forward. This might be the first night sleep for them in a long time, he hoped.

All the time the Sargent was keeping the commanders at the headquarters abreast of what was going on. He was told to keep his men there at this town for a couple of days and see what the Germans next move was going to be. He also told the Sargent to be ready to move out in a moment's notice if they came back. He also told everyone to keep his equipment very close by to be ready to move quickly without being told.

Right after dark the shelling from the Germans started to fall all over the little town. The Sarge lost a few men before they could get out of town a little ways.

This Lasted for nearly four hours and then it stopped again. It caught everyone off guard and the head brass could not figure why they would want back into this little town. But all they wanted to do was to place a few snippers in the town so they could do their job.

After waiting for a short period of time the Sargent ordered his men to move back into town and try to get some rest. During the night a couple of snipers moved back into town without the men knowing anything was going on. It was the first time that he men had rested for a few hours like this in days so they took advantage of it. As the sun began to break the hill overlooking the town the men began to rise and look around at where they were at. The Sarge came to the middle of the street and ordered the men to move out in thirty minutes, then as he turns to go up the street a single shot rang out and hits the Sargent right in the chest. It seemed to be what the sniper was waiting on was for a high official to get to where he could pick him off and this was his opportunity to do it.

Willie was the closest person to the Sargent so he ran to get him from the street when another shot rang out and hit Willie in the lower part of his shoulder. By this time the men saw where the shots were coming from and they open fire with a machine gun on the window and the man fell half way out the window. Then two of the men ran and got Willie by the legs and dragged him to cover into a building to where the medics could stop the bleeding and patch his shoulder up.

Willie was in terrible pain at this time and the medics gave him something the pain and started to bandage the shoulder up so they could get him back to the staging area and then to a hospital somewhere. Most of the time Willie was out cold from the medicine they gave him for the pain. As they were loading him up he men said,

"Boy are you lucky, you are getting to go home after a week over here, and we will probably be here forever."

All that Willie could do was grin at them and then close his eyes again for the pain. The ride back to the ground hospital was rough and muddy. All the way he thought that he was going to die. He thought about the wedding he was going to have with Morning Dove. He was thinking how this was going to go down the drain. He had not even had time to write his mother and tell her what his address was or how she could get in touch with him.

As he reached the field hospital, he was talking out of his head about the wedding about his mother about the chief in the village and all the things that had taken place back home. He kept wondering to his self if he was going to die or not. Would his mother get his body to be buried on the reservation?

As he lay there through the night h, he began to listen to the major talking about the way the Germans could decode the messages that they would send and know where to hit the convoy that would be bringing their supplies to them. They could not see how they could decode it that fast. He often wondered if they had spies in their camp, but he knew different.

Major Patillo would send all kind of messages to the men that would be shipping their supplies. He would even send decoys, but they would not be bothered, they would be let through. Why. This was the thing that was bothering him. It was his job to figure out how to get the supplies through. He even went to the old children's talk they did back home, it was called pig Latin, but the Germans knew exactly what it was also.

The Major had studied this kind of talk for years in Washington D.C in the military spy ring. He was even a spy at one time trying to figure out some of the language that they were talking to confuse the country, it was his job to try and figure it all out. Now the army needs his help here in Germany so that they would have enough supplies to fight the war.

Willie and some of the other men are loaded in an ambulance to be trucked to the nearest airport, which was twelve miles away and then he was to be flown to a little town north of Rome where they would evaluate his shoulder and see what would be the next step to take. It was not a bad ride because they were getting away from where the shells had fallen on the road then after that he would be put on the plane and to the hospital.

Upon arriving at the hospital his pain was a lot less now since the medication had a few days to take hold. Willie got to thinking about what the boys had said back at the front lines, that now he would be getting to go home, but he was wondering when and what shape. The doctors and the nurses had been coming in very regularly giving him all kind of medication. He would ask them where he was at and they would say you are just outside of Rome Italy at the military hospital.

He had a good night rest that night with all the medicine that they had given him and all the sleep that he had lost in the last week. After he had a good breakfast the next morning, there came in his room three doctors. Two of them were a lot older than the young one. They had a set of x-rays that they had taken of his shoulder and they hung then upon the wall in the frame that was on the wall and told him to look at them as they went over them with him. One of the X-rays showed very clearly that that the bullet had cut right through the bone of the arm right below where it connected to the shoulder itself. They went and explained to him that the arm would no longer be of any use to him even if they left it on and that it would probably give him trouble the rest of his life, so their recommendation was that they remove the arm at the shoulder, but they was going to leave it up to him because he was the one that was going to have to live with it the rest of his life.

All the time the doctors had been talking to Willie they could see the tears starting to build up in his eyes, then it finally reached the point to where his cheeks were covered with tears. They turned to leave one of them said "we will be back later on today and see if you have made that decision."

Willie lay there in his bed and wondered how he could live with just one arm, and yet he had seen men live with no legs and no arms so if they could then he could do the same. Then he got to wondering what would his mother say, would Morning dove still want him. All these thoughts came in his mind as he lay there that day thinking what to tell the doctors. Finally about three 'clock that day the doctors came back in to his room to talk to him again and see if he had made some kind of a decision.

"Well son we have studied the X-rays again and we still have come to the same conclusion. It's something that is hard to say and it is not easy on our side either, but we know the trouble you will have later on in life if it is still there" the older doctor said

"Doc. How can I write and tell my mother what has happen to me. Do you think she will understand?" Willie asked

"If your mother is like the other hundred mothers whose son this same thing has happened, they were probably like your mother, they will understand." The doctor said again then he continued "son they took your arm but you still will have your life and what you make out of it will be all up to you, so tomorrow we will operate if that is all right."

"That will be fine doctor, but I need to write my mother and tell her what has happened to me and things will be a little different when I get home, but how can I write like this now." He asked

"I will send you in a nurse after you eat your supper and you can tell her what to write son" and she will send it off for you and everything. How will that be son." He asked

"That will be fine sir, thank you very much." Said Willie

After supper they sent a Red Cross nurse in to write the letter for him. She made it clear to him what he said would not go no further than that room. Whatever he wanted to say it would be put in the letter and sent to his mother. As Willie started talking the nurse started to writing. He talked for a long time and then he was getting sleepy and told her that would be all he would write this time. By the time he got the address and got it ready to mail Willie was already fast asleep.

The next morning before Willie was fully awake they give him a pain relaxer and it almost put him back to sleep. Then they put his either mask on to put him out and headed him to the operating room. The operation lasted a little over four house and then they kept him sedated for most of the day and he slept the rest of the night. Nurses checking on him constantly to make sure that he would not come to all of a sudden

The next day he woke up bright and early and the nurse standing right there with him and asked him how he felt and he told her he was feeling fine. She asked him about his pain and he said it was very little.

"if that pain comes back we want to know, the doctor said for us to keep it down as much as possible, so you tell me if it starts to get worse." The nurse said.

"Yes ma'am I will let you know, thank you so much." Willie said

For the next week he just lay in bed and about every few hours he would walk down the hall and see some of the other men that had the same condition that he had. In the room two doors down from his room, across the hall they kept the door shut but every now and then he could hear someone yell something, but with the door shut he could not make out what they was saying. But one night when his nurse came in he asked her what was going on in the room across the hall with the door shut all the time. She said

"he was just brought in three days ago with a very bad leg wound, at first the doctors thought they would remove it but now they have changed their minds and they are going to leave it on we are just trying to keep the pain down after his surgery like we did for you" then she turned and left the room.

Sometime during the day one of the nurses came to the room across the hall and left the door open until she had taken all of her vital signs and then when she left the room she left the door open again by mistake because he had told them to keep it shut. After about thirty minutes he would yell at the nurses, "shut my door, hey you shut my door.'" And then this one time he let out a yell that nobody in the hospital recognized except Willie. It was the native tongue of the tribe of Indians that all of Willies people used back home. Who is this he thought.

Willie, in his native tongue yelled back, "Hey you let us keep it quiet over there." There was complete silence for at least five minutes before the voice came back from the other room, "have I died and gone to heaven and some angel is speaking to me in my native tongue, I would like to see this angel and shake his hand." Was the answer from the other room?

Willie had quietly gotten out of his bed and walked to the room and was trying to see who it was in the room, then all of a sudden it dawned on his that the only other Native American was lone wolf from the same tribe he came from. So instead of just slowly going in he burst in and there was lone wolf laying there with his leg all hiked up in the air with a cast on it.

"What happen to you friend, it don't look like the same thing that happen to me. " Willie said

"No I got hit by a mortar round and I tried to get away when it struck me in the leg, and here I am laying here waiting to go home. Lone wolf said

"Maybe we will get to go home together in a few weeks." Willie responded. About that time the nurse came by and told Willie to get to his room because they had lone wolf isolated for a few days to keep down infection from visitors.

For the next few days they laid in their bed and talked to each other across the hall in their native tongue. They would talk hours on hours about the times back home about the fighting. One day while they were talking they had not noticed that Major Patillo had walked by them talking in their native tongue. He paused for just a moment and then went on to see one of his commanders that had been hit the same time that lone wolf had been hit.

While the major was in the commander's room they talked about the Germans knowing every move that the convoy was doing. They were wondering how they could decode all the messages that they sent through. The major was there with him trying to figure out what they were going to do. After about an hour with him the Major left the room and started down the hall and passed Willie and lone wolf talking in their native tongue to each other. He stopped in the hall for just a few minutes and then went on to the front and out of the hospital.

The next day he came back to the hospital to say good bye to his commander on down the hall from Willie and Lone Wolf. When he got to their room they were talking again and he stopped to listen again to them talk in their native tongue. He continues on down hall to where he was going and as he entered he said to the Commander "I think I have found the answer to our decoding problem. "Before he could finish what he was going to tell him, the doctor and nurse came in for their visit with him.

Major Patillo asked the doctor "Doc is there any way I can push him down the hall for just a minute with your help it will be just around the corner."

"Well don't think it will hurt that much, there is nothing hooked to him now, you lead the way to where you want to go" the doctor said and they began to push till they reached the edge of Willies room and they stopped and just listened. After about five minutes they took him back to his room and the Major asked him "what do you think"

"We'll let us talk to them" he said. The doctor and the nurse walked out of the room and they talked about it for a few minutes and thought how they were going to get the two together with them.

"I will get you a wheel chair and push you down to the room and we can meet in the room across the hall and introduce ourselves. I will make it alright with the doctor before I bring the chair to get you" Major Patillo said. In about fifteen minutes he returns with the chair and loads the commander in it and down the hall they go to Willies room first.

The boys are still talking to each other and the two officers just stopped outside of Willies room and listen for a while and then the major walked into Willies room and introduced himself and then told him that he had somebody that he wanted him to meet. He pushes the wheel chair in to his room and introduces him to Willie and ask him who is that across the hall that he is talking to, and Willie tells them who it is and they ask him if they could all go over there and talk to them to.

"Have we done something wrong sir? We are just talking in our native tongue because it is so much easier than the English language." Willie ask.

"No the major, on the contrary we think it is wonderful and we want to talk to you about it." And then they headed over to lone wolfs room across the hall and he sees the officers and he did not know what to do. He raised his hand in salute position and the major told him that was alright this time it was an informal meeting.

"We come here to make you boys a proposition. We want you to stay in the army a little longer. Now that might be confusing to you two, but I want you to hear me out and then see what you think." The major said and he then went on and tried to explain to the boys how that the Germans knew every move they made with their convoy carrying their necessary equipment, like food, equipment and so on. They know how to decode all of our messages as soon as they get them.

He told them how they wanted them to be one at one station and the other at the other and tell the men what each other says. They would go up in rank and their pay would increase and their muster out pay would be larger and they would get a large, pay increase also just for staying for a little longer and see if the Germans could interpret what they were saying. All you boys will do is sat behind a desk for the remainder of time until you get ready to leave, but now we need your help.

"It will be a few days before you get out, so that will give you time to think about it. I will still be in and out for the next few days. I want you boys to think about it if you will." The major said and he turns and pushes the chair back down the hall.

The boys sat for a few minutes in silence before lone wolf spoke up and said "Well I don't guess that

I have nothing to do for the next few months, I guess that I will try it if you will."

"The pay raise sounds good to me and it means more on my disability when I get out and that will help on me buying the piece of ground I want to buy and build a house on, I guess we just as well try it for a little while and see what becomes of it." Willie said then he turns and walks out of the room and tells lone wolf that he is going to write his mother a letter and try to explain the situation to them and tell them about the raises that it will mean to them and that he would not be in any fighting any more.

The boys found out that there was about only two convoys a week that they had to get through and the major told them every now and then they could talk to each other just to try to confuse the Germans. At the Germans headquarters they were completely confused at the language that the Americans were using, they just wondered if it was some kind of trick that they were doing, and yet at the American headquarters they were very well pleased at what Willie and Lone Wolf had done for them.

After a little over a year their replacements arrived and now they would take over till the war was over and the Germans never did break the code the boys were using. And it was only the true American language.

Willie goes back to his barracks and sat down and wrote a letter and told his mother about what time he would be home and the women were very excited because it had been a little over two years since they saw him and now it was time. The boys in the next few days took care of all their paper work, took care of their pension pay and all the rest that they would have coming to them. Willie would be getting enough for his arm to buy that piece of ground that he and Morning Dove wanted that was on the reservation and they would have enough to start their house also.

Judith had not told Willie that she had been working at the factory for a little over a year to help them build that house they wanted, she had not told him that she had purchased a car and that Morning Dove and her had learned to drive it so when she heard what time they would be getting at the county seat, they would drive up to meet them and surprise them. The Major at the fort told Judith what time they would be getting off the train at the county seat that was all the women wanted to know.

On the day of their arrival, Judith had taken off work so she and Morning Dove could be there at the train depot to greet them. So they left early that morning, for the boys would arrive at eight o'clock that morning. They were very nervous for they had not seen him without his arm, they did not know how that he would react to them looking at him. As they sat with the windows down in the car, finally they heard the train whistle blow at the edge of town. Judith could feel the sweat in her hands getting worse. She did not know if she needed to get out or just sat there till he got off the train.

Morning Dove looked over at Judith and she could see the tears building up in her eyes and she could feel the same thing in hers also. Finally Morning Dove says "Let us just sit her until we see them get off the train for the bus will not be here for another two hours and they will be just walking around and we will walk up and surprise them.

The train was pulling into the station when the women looked at each other and burst into tears. They were in such a commotion that they had not noticed that the train had stopped and the boys were getting off and looking around to where they would go and wait on the bus. Just as they started to sit down on a bench Willie turned around and saw Morning Dove get out of this car and come running to where he was and grabbed him and kissed him and cried on his shoulder till Judith had to wait her turn.

Finally Judith grabbed him and would not turn him loose for a long time. Morning Dove turned to lone wolf and gave him a long hug also. By this time Judith turns him loose and turns to lone wolf also and does him the same way. Then Morning Dove said "we'll let us go home and get out of these people way so they can get on the train".

"Don't we have to wait on the bus for a ride" Willie ask

"No our ride is right over here" Judith spoke up

"Well where did this come from and who drives it" Willie ask

"It is mine and we both drives it. I drive it to work and she drives it to get things" Judith says

"Well I hope you two know what you are doing, let us go home lone wolf and see what else has changed" Willie said as they got their duffel bag and loaded them into the car and headed home. On the way home it was talk about what the girls had been doing and what changes had taken place since they had been gone, and about Judith working at the factory where they make bullets and other war material. In the two hour ride it was nothing but talk about what each other had been doing all the time that they had be separated.

When they arrived at their home, Lone Wolfs father was there waiting on him, for the women told him that he was coming home with Willie and they would pick him up when they did willie. His father was very proud to see him, just like the women was to see Willie.

"You two just go riding around or just do what you want to do for a little while and I will us something to eat." Judith said

"Mom you just do what you want to do, all I want to do is just sit here and look at the country side. I have not seen this in about two years. And I want to see Morning Dove and talk to her". It was a wonderful time as they sat and talked to each other about what was going to take place. Willie wanted to go see the chief about the ground he wanted to buy at the back of the reservation. If he could purchase it from the tribe then he would be free from all the taxation that the government would impose on them living off the reservation.

It was not long until Judith came and yelled for them to come and eat a bite. They had been walking down the road holding hands and talking about their marriage. They thought they would go to the chief and see what time would be a good time for him to marry them. Willie ask if he could drive her to work tomorrow and she informed him that she would ride the military bus that took the employees to work that wanted to ride it and then would bring them back home that evening.

He told her what he wanted to see the chief for so she told them they could take their car. Then after eating them all sat and talked as the time passed off fast and Judith told them she was going to bed so she could go to work in the morning. Morning Dove had his room already fixed for him so all he had to do was go get in bed, and she had laid her cover out by the sofa.

The next morning when he awoke from his tiresome sleep he could smell the bacon cooking on the stove so he hurried and got dressed in his civilian clothes so he could look like he was out of the army. He told Morning dove that he wanted to stop and see the new Major in the army there at the fort. Then they would go to see the chief on the reservation.

When he went in to see the Major he told him that his name was Willie Anderson and that he just got home and he wanted to see the new Major that was here now. When he introduced himself to the major, the major said "Yes I know about you and the time you had in the army, and was not there another recruit with you also."? The major asked

"Yes sir that was lone wolf. We were wounded a few days apart and ended up in the same hospital before we came home." Willie replied then he told the major that all he wanted to do was to just stop and say hello and would like to come down some time and just sat and talk when he had time to put up with him. As Willie was leaving the major told him to drop by anytime and they would talk.

The next stop was on the reservation. It had changed quite a bit because some of the people had started working at the factory and then they bought one of the government ome3s and moved off the reservation. They parked down at the entrance and walked in to the chief's tepee and one of his braves came to meet them and he asked them what they wanted and he told him he wanted to see the chief. Who do I tell him is here, Willie told him to tell him Willie is here?

When the chief came out and saw who it was he grabbed Willie and gave him a big bear hug and then all of a sudden backed off and said "Oh I'm sorry Willie I did not know this has happened to you. Then Willie explained to him how it happened. They sat and talked for a while and then Willie told him why he was there.

"As far as the wedding, that is up to you two. You set the date on this." The chief replied and then he added "What else can I help you with."

"We want a piece of ground on the back side of the reservation, we would like to buy it to build a home on. Chief Katawas was talking very favorable about it when I left. We want to raise our children on the reservation like in the olden days."

"I see no problem with it myself, but I will bring it up to the council and see what they think and let you know before your wedding Saturday." The chief said

"If they agree to it can we sit up our tepee this Saturday on the ground and stay there for our honeymoon."? Willie ask

Then the chief said "I think ever thing is on go for you two." The chief said as he turned and walked back into his tepee

Judith knew that they were going to be married as soon he got home from the army so she started to making him his wedding clothes while he was in the army and Morning Dove already had her clothes ready also, so all she needed to do was to pack some cooking utensils and sleeping blankets for the tepee. They had made it ok to use the car for a little while, until he got his checks from the army going and his disability check from the government, then they would buy their own car. Their home would be started in a few days and they would try to be in it before winter.

Saturday came and everyone was dressed in their bright color. It was beautiful all the way through. Tears was flowing everywhere. The women had brought gifts for her to cook with and some of them brought blankets to cover with. Everything that they needed was given to them. After the weeding and Willie and Morning Dove started for their ground that the council said they could have for a small price the braves of the chief was right on their tails with their horses.

Willie was wondering what they were going to do when they got there and it did not take them very lone to find out. All the braves got busy and in a matter of minutes they had the tepee sat up and was on the back to the chief's tepee. The chief had done this as a wedding present.

Things went pretty well as planned for the completion of their house. To Morning Dove it was looking like a castle to her. She had running water in the kitchen so she had a sink also, and she thought that was wonderful. They had given Judith's car back to her and got one of their own.

It as a week after they moved into their house that the Major at the fort came to see Willie and asked him to be at the fort on Saturday morning at nine o'clock sharp and Willie told him he would be there. He could not figure out why, but he had learned to ask why later so he was to be there whatever the situation.

When he got there Saturday at nine o'clock the first one he saw was lone wolf standing in front of the office building. As he started up to the building there came major Sanders, major Patillo, and the new Major that was there now Major Emory all coming out of the building and standing at attention and when Willie got to Lone Wolf all the Majors turned to them and gave them a big salute and the boys gave them one back

Neither one of the boys had noticed the statue of an army man that was vailed on the way in by the walkway. Major Patillo stood and read how that these two men saved more lives than most soldiers ever thought about saving, by getting their convoy through the enemy lines until their relief came. This statue is in memory of these two men and their name will be forever engraved on i.e. are thankful to Lone Wolf and to Willie Anderson for a job well done.

After all the celebration Willie and Morning Dove went back to their home feeling very rewarded. They are still there today in Willie Anderson's mind.

Thank you
Ray Sowell

THE RIVER

Here in this little settlement of Cabool, a very quiet little parish that lies on the northern end of Mexico a river run the length of the whole town. The river means nothing to most of the residents that live here. To some of the others it means a way of a different life. It means a living for their families through the winter months. It is a paradise for them if they can go over to work on the other side.

To this young man that have lived his entire life here in Cabool he is determined to leave here and go over this river even if it cost him his life. The only thing that he sees here in this small village is there is no pave streets, the sand blows most of the time. There is hardly no rain fall here during the summer months. The soil can hardly grow 'any kind of vegetation.

The thing that usually grows here is the short cactus that dots the landscape. About the only tree that you can see grows at the river's edge. Some of them are small, others like the cottonwood grows quite tall.

Most every day about sun down a young man can be seen walking along the bank to the river always looking to the other side of the river. The young man's name is Juan Sanchez. Ever since he had lost one of his best friends a few years back, he had a determination to go to the land of promise that be thinks is on the other side of the river.

His mother is usually at home doing some kind of work around the home, to keep the place looking like a home. Juan is a senior in his high school. All he thinks about is the opportunity that will come his way to go across the river to work.

His mother has been supporting him for the past twelve years by herself to send him to school. She has picked up a job of ironing for the influential people that have moved here to get away from the large city life and the drug cartel that stays there.

Maria remembers the night that Juan's father Manuel, left to go across the river to try to work at one of the produce farms across the river and he never returned home, nor has he ever been heard of since. They have tried to locate him through the Red Cross but to no avail.

Maria went and signed up for a subsidy check from the government to get Juan through school.

But she had to take in the laundry to get him through and pay all the bills.

Juan was five years old at the time his father went to look for work. He and other men had been planning on going for a Jong time. He remembers that some of the men came back the same night or the next day, but his dad never returned.

As Juan was growing up he would go to the men and asked them about his father, but they would tell him they never seen him after they crossed the river, they did not know what happened to him. They would tell him that some were caught out in the dessert, while others made it back to the river, then there was a few that made it to the mesquite grove, where no body hardly ever comes out of it.

Most of the time the U.S.Officials would not even go into the grove of trees and the cactus to get anyone, thinking that no one could make it out alive. He also had heard some of the men talking about the night that his dad came up missing how that he and another man made it into the mesquite grove, but that was the last time anyone heard of them, or even saw them.

Juan would listen to the men talk because one day him and his friend "Rio", who was in school with him would one day go across the river. They were waiting for the time that they were both out of school, and they would find out all they could to prepare themselves for the trip.

As he would walk along that river bank. All he could do was to dream of that time he could go and work and make a living for his mother, but he knew that time was not yet.

Him and Rio would meet and walk the river bank day after day and talk about how they would try to get across the desert on the other side without being caught.

One Friday afternoon while they were in school Juan yelled to Rio, "hey Rio, let's go swimming tomorrow about noon in the river at the hole.

"Ok" Rio yelled back, "1 will meet you about noon at the river." Juan threw up his hand to motion that he would be there.

When he reached home he says to his mother, "mom, Rio wants me to go swimming with him tomorrow about noon, will that be all right."

"Yes "she said "You just don't stay to long so that I will have to come looking for you." Maria just kept ironing the clothes she was working on to get them finished for the weekend. She was trying to get done to have grocery money for the weekend.

Juan did not ever realize the hardship that he and his mother faced from month *to* month. Just to send him to school took all she made for the ironing. Then the little check she drew from the government paid her bills to where there was only a small amount left. Juan knew they did not have money for sodas, candy and things like that. He knew he had to do without them while the other kids bad them.

That was his dream, to one day to cross that river and make enough money to afford things of this nature.

The next day Juan started toward the river to go swimming with Rio just like he told him he would. It was only a short distant to the river from his home. When he arrived there at the hole, there was Rio already in the water splashing around. "Hurry up and come on in "he yelled.

"I will be there right away, just give me a moment to change my clothes "Juan said. As he jumped behind some bushes to change into a pair of shorts to swim in. "Here I come "as he jumped from the cliff into the water, almost hitting Rio in the head as he hit the water. "How long have you been here" as he came up out of the water.

"About thirty minutes ago" Rio replied.

As they swam and jumped from the cliff yelling and screaming as they hit the water, they looked across the river and there was a ranger with a pair of binoculars trying to see who all was there and see if they would stay on their side of the river.

The ranger was setting in his truck on a small weedy hill overlooking the swimming hole. He would not intimidate anyone that was in the water playing around, but you Jet someone try to cross for any reason he would be there in a minute.

Juan saw him first and raised his hand to wave to him, just to let him know they knew that he was there. The ranger waved back as if to say hello to the boys. He had seen the boys every time they were a the hole swimming.

Rio saw Juan wave to him and said, "hey, let's go over and talk to the ranger". "You know we can't do that. He would take is in and arrest us, and no telling what he would do to us." Juan replied. "I am planning on finishing going to school, you know I only have a few weeks to go, l am not going to mess it up doing something like this. I am going to wait till then before r go across the river, then we will get us a job when we go across.

"Yea he probably would, but one day I am going to go over there and see what is on the other side of the river for myself." Rio says

"I have heard old men talk about going over and working to make a living for their family to live on then they would return after the work was done, but now they talk about how hard it is to go over because of the rangers like him up and down the river. "Juan said "they do not know if the U.S has made new laws keeping people like us or what, they do not know.

Someday, or some night we will go in the dark when there will be a good moon to travel by "Rio said,

"I am going to go over in a few days or more, on a field trip from school. The teacher sent home to my mother telling her when we were to go and what we were going to see. Do not want to do anything to mess that trip up.

"Will you *try* to hide somewhere and not come back home this time" Rio asked

"NO", said Juan "I will be watched very carefully, and I will have someone watching me all the time. I won't have an opportunity to get away this time. We had better go home so we can let the ranger rest and go to his home also.

Juan went back behind the bushes and changed in to his dry clothes, then as the boys started home they turned again to the ranger and gave him another wave lust to say goodbye and he returned the wave. As Juan rode his bike toward his home, he could not but help to look across the river just to catch a glimpse of what was on the other side of the river.

The Mexico side of the river was a little higher than the American side. When the rainy season came and the water got to flood stage, it would flood the other side of the river before Juan and Maria had to move out to higher ground.

The boys finally go to where they had to say goodbye to each other for the day, Rio started down the road to his home, then turned and yelled to Juan, "see you at mass in the morning bright and early,"

"I'll be there if I can" He yelled back. He continues on his bike toward home still thinking what is on the America side of the river.

Maria was in the kitchen when Juan arrives at home. He walks into the kitchen where his mom was fixing taco's for supper, this was a common meal for poor people in this little province " Mom "he asks "what do you think the other side of the river looks like, how many miles do the desert run across it".

Almost in a surprise way she says, "Well I have never seen it myself. but l have talked to a few women and some men who have been there for a while and they say there is places where the people have to cut their grass with machjnes it keep it smooth as a rug and it stays green almost all year round.

Sometimes they even put water on it to make it grow.

The roads almost everywhere is black and hard as they can be. They have little dust, except when the wind blows, then we all have it."

Standing across the table from Juan, she sees a look of bewilderment, someone who cannot understand what had just been said, but she turns to Juan and asks "why do you ask". He sat there for a moment then he says "oh I was just wandering what I was going to see when I go on my field trip in a few weeks."

Maria knew down in her heart the main reason why he ask a question like this. She knew that someday he would do the same thing that his dad had tried.

Juan had never told her that Rio and he had been talking about trying to go to the fan fields someday. It was just a matter of time.

Before he had time to get up from the table Maria says, "You were too small to remember the last time your father and some of the other men plotted for days how they were going to go work in the fields to make extra money for the winter that was the last time I ever saw him. The plan that he and the other men worked on for so long must to not have gone like it was supposed to go.

"He never did tell you what he expected to find when he got to where he was going. He did not know how hard the work was going to be. "Be asked.

"No, He just talked about how they would travel by night in small groups, that way if some got caught some of the others would have a better chance of making it to where they were going. He said some of the other men that he talked to that had come back after being lost in the desert for days said that they would run upon bones of someone who had died trying to make it across, maybe they ran out of water, maybe they got rattlesnake bit, and maybe there was a dozen of other reasons why they did not make it across. I wish now he had never had tried to go and work in the fields, maybe this would never had happen to him. Some of the women have been waiting for years for their husbands, their boys to come home, but it has never happened, just like your father, who has been gone all of these years. We will never know what has happen to him. Maybe he wanted to keep the wages for his own self, maybe he found another woman and had to spend all he made on her, I guess we will never know, maybe some of those bones in the dessert belongs to him, "she says

"Mom, "Juan says "someday I want to go over and try to find work, you know that we need help through the winter when we have to keep warm, maybe I can find dad and see where he is at."

"We are doing just fine "she says, "I do not want to lose a son like I lost a husband and never see him also. I do not want to hear no more about this, you just go ahead and sat at the table and we will eat in just a moment.

'Ok mom," he said as he got up to get the plates and the hardware to eat with also, then he turned and walked out the door for just a breath of fresh air, waiting for her to holler supper. He just wanted to look across the river another time. He could not keep his eyes from the other side of the river, during of the day he would be able to go over and work for a living on someone's farm. He wanted for his mother to have things she had done without for all the years she had to send him to school. Every dime she would make extra went for bills of some kind. He just wanted to pay her back, and this is the only way he knew how to do it

The next morning when the son was just peaking over the horizon, Juan jumped up, grabbed his Sunday clothes to go meet Rio at mass. It was always a pair of shorts, his blue shirt and the floppy old sandals that he always wore to mass. The other day through the week usually was barefooted. His feet had become as tough as the side on the old donkeys back that lived across the road.

The bells on the steeple of the church had started ringing. He stuck his head in the doorway, let out a yell to his mother, "Mom I am going to mass, I will be back later.

"Ok "she yelled back ' 'you come home soon afterward", but he was already running down the road to meet his friend Rio.

It was only a short distance to the church, so he could run all the way and not even be breathing hard when he got there, He spotted Rio, and he gave him a big wave and yelled to him, "how long have you been here, "he asked as he came closed to him.

"About ten minutes or so is all, 1 could not sleep, so I got up because it was so hot and just ate a bite of breakfast and came on down here", he replied.

They stood outside for a little while talking to each other, then the people began to go in so they went in with them. They sat quietly during the services, but when the service was over they ran like a wild boar was after them. They get outside and both of them are about out of breath when Rio speaks, up "let's go swimming again today. The weather is so hot we can cool of in the water, maybe we can wave at the ranger sitting across the river."

"I will go home and ask my mother. I know that it will be after we eat. If she says yes I will meet you a little after dinner, and then l will meet you at the hole. "Juan said.

"I will be there waiting on you. Rio says, as he waves a good bye to him he gets on his bike and heads for the swimming hole.

Rio was not tied down with a tight rein like Juan was. His mother bad died when was about five years of age, about the time that Juan lost his dad, his father did not do a good job of raising him. The only good thing that the father had done was to make him get him an education so he could get a good job when he left home. The father rule was not the same kind of rule the mother had with Juan. Rio could come and go almost as he pleased. If his father gave him something to do, and he did not want to do it, he would just go outside of the house for a while until his father would do the job for him. He had got mixed up with the drug people at times, but we could always manage somehow to slip away from them before he got arrested.

Juan had warned him that if he was to be his friend that he was going to have to leave the drug people alone or else he would have nothing to do with him, and so far he had heeded that warning, he had left them alone.

Juan knew too well what those drugs could do for you. He had a very close friend a few years back, before he met Rio, a boy by the name of Carlos Warez. They had become the best of friends. He would take him fishing, swimming or wherever he wanted to go. He was a few years older than Juan, and that was the thing that troubled Maria, yet he was a very likeable person for her and for him, it just seemed like a friend that you would like for your son to be with.

There was very few people that you could pick for a friend in this part of the country. He had graduated three years before Juan was to complete school. He had left for a while and then came back, no one knew where he went or what he did while he was gone. But it seemed that he would always have a little money when he came home.

Maria liked Carlos, she had known his family for a number of years. His family would look after Maria when they saw Juan's father was not going to come back from across the river.

When Carlos would come back from one of his trips, he would always head for the store and come home with a soda and a bag of peanuts poured in the bottle over the soda.

Juan and Maria never knew what exactly happened to Carlos the day the police found him lying in one of the streets about sun up one morning. He had been shot four times in the chest and the head. In the police report it was stated that he must to have been shot out of town, and the body thrower in the street by some drug gang.

For months after that, Juan would not hardly talk to anyone about Carlos to anyone. He was a big boy, but not big enough to take on the drug people, if that is what happened.

Then one day while he was at school, all down hearted, thin king about what had happened a few weeks before, about Carlos, the only friend he had in the world, this young boy went over to him just to talk to him. At first Juan would not say anything to him, but Rio insisted that he should put a smile on his face, lift his head up and enjoy life.

Juan just could not but to help and put a smile on his face, then the two started talking to each, and from that day to this they have been the best of friends. Juan thinking here was a small boy, nothing compared to Carlos in stature, wanting somebody to be friends with.

Carlos was still in the mind of Juan almost every day. He could remember him coming to town with a few dollars in his pocket, Juan did not know where it came from, and he never did ask him about it.

When he would talk to him about going across the river to get a job and work, all he would say to him was "there is good money over here on this side of the river. If you cross the river you have to work all day for little to nothing.

Juan did not like for him to talk about America like that, because he knew that it was the land of promise.

The only problem was trying to cross the river and get where the work was at. He could still remember him buying himself that soda and the bag of peanuts and pouring them in the bottle, then drinking them. He thought that was a wonderful drink to have and one day when he get across the river he was going to have himself one of them.

Now Juan starts home from mass hoping that his mother has dinner ready because he is thinking how hungry that he is, yet he knows it is a little early for dinner to be fixed, so he just takes his time, picking up a rock now and then throwing them, into the river that he has done for years now. He gets close enough to his home to see his mother out in the yard washing the windows that had collected dust from the traffic on the main road, yet the wind could carry it all over town.

This town of Cobos, the main streets ran along the river, it was the one that was traveled the most, and the smaller streets ran north and south. On the north side of town was the river that ran through the town, on the south side there was mountains everywhere. Juan and Maria lived by the river on the north side of town while Rio and his father lived on the south side of town. The school house was on Main Street.

There was less than forty students in the whole school from the first to the twelfth grade.

The younger people would move out as soon as they got out of school, or they would get married and move to the larger cities to work for their living, sometimes coming back and get their fathers and mothers to come and live with them.

The people that Maria worked for had built their home here to escape the Government taxing on residents in the larger cities. They also wanted to escape the drug wars that was beginning to take over certain parts of the city. The merchants that was still in business here in Cobos had to pay a certain tax, they knew it for the support of the drug people, but it still had to be paid just the same, if you refused you may come up missing or you be burned out as one was done.

The town had one constable or policeman. His bands were tied when it came to the drug people.

He was there mostly for peaceful disturbance. That was all that he handled.

"Juan come in and eat its ready," his mom yelled He was setting on the river bank behind the house. Every day he was dreaming when he could cross the river and see what it was like over on the other said.

To eat.

Remember him buying himself that soda and the bag of peanuts and pouring them in the bottle, then drinking them. He thought that was a wonderful drink to have and one day when he get across the river he was going to have himself one of them.

Now Juan starts home from mass hoping that his mother has dinner ready because he is thinking how hungry that he is, yet he knows it is a l little early for dinner to be fixed, so he just takes his time, picking up a rock now and then throwing them, into the river that he has done for years now. He gets close enough to his home to see his mother out in the yard washing the windows that had collected dust from the traffic on the main road, yet the wind could carry it all over town.

Though this town of Cobos, the main streets ran along the river, it was the one that was traveled the most, the smaller streets ran north and south. On the north side of town was the river that ran through the town, on the south side there was mountains everywhere. Juan and Maria lived by the river on the north side of town while Rio and his father lived on the south side of town. The school house was on Main Street.

There was less than forty students in the whole school from the first to the twelfth grade.

The younger people would move out as soon as they got out of school, or they would get married and move to the larger cities to work for their living, sometimes coming back and get their fathers and mothers to come and live with them.

The people that Maria worked for had built their home here to escape the Government taxing on residents in the larger cities. They also wanted to escape the drug wars that was beginning to take over certain parts of the city. The merchants that was still in business here in Cobos had to pay a certain tax, they knew it for the support of the drug people, but it still had to be paid just the same, if you refused you may come up missing or you be burned out as one was done.

The town had one constable or policeman. His bands were tied when it came to the drug people.

He was there mostly for peaceful disturbance. That was all that he handled.

"Juan come in and eat its ready," his mom yelled He was setting on the river bank behind the house. Every day he was dreaming when he could cross the river and see what it was like over on the other side

Get to her. She would have to check with western union from time to time to see if anything had come for her.

This one afternoon Manuel was working in the yard, Maria was doing laundry for her family. As she started from the washing machine she noticed in the comer behind the machine, there was something there that had never been there before. It was crammed in the comer where you could not see it unless you just happen to look in the right place.

There was a back pack, a pair of boots, and a large straw hat. She would not go over and examine it, she knew what it was for, she'd not know when, or how soon. She would wait and see if he would tell her about it or not.

Later that afternoon Maria was gathering he clothes from the outside line to bring into the house, when she saw Manuel talking to two men for a long time, then they left and waved at him and said their good bee's when they left.

She goes into the house and lays her laundry out so she could iron what was needed for the next few days.

The sun had gone down now and the darkness had come over the whole town, the moon was coming up in the east, it put a little light on this small town.

As she was ironing, Manuel came in from the outside. He stopped across from the ironing board as if he wanted to say something to her, but instead he leaned over and kissed her and told her he was going to go to bed.

Back in Maria mind she knew that tonight was the night. Words would not come to her to try to stop him. She knew that he loved her and she loved him. She also knew that the family always came first with him, and he thought this was what he needed to do to support his family. She knew that there were no jobs in the big cities because that is where everyone was going to make a living for their families.

When she finally got to go to bed she found Manuel already asleep, so she thought, well maybe this is not the night because he is already asleep, and maybe he won't wake up till morning. Feeling somewhat at ease, she to lays down and began pondering things in her mind. Question of all kind she kept asking herself, with no answers.

Sometimes later she falls asleep only to be awaken up by someone in the house moving around. She reaches over to awake Manuel when the front door closes, and she could not find him in bed. She knew it was him leaving. She sat on the side of the bed looking at two men standing by the side of the road waiting for him to reach then, then all would head for the river.

Tears began to roll down her cheeks as she sat and watch them go over the river bank. She lay back on her pillow still crying, wondering if she would ever see him again. What was going to happen to her and Juan? How was she going to send him to school, How would she pay her bills, These things she could not answer, she did not know.

For the next few days all she could was to ponder the thoughts of him being gone. Did he get over and go to work. Could he send money to her? What was going to happen to him when the work ran out, all these things was on her mind. She did not want to think of moving to a large city and try to find a job just to support Juan and her. She did not like the idea of going to work in the factories because of what she had heard of how the women were treated that worked there and if you did not play alone with them you did not work for very long.

It had been little over a week now since he left home. She thought that when Juan was in school she would walk down to store and get some beans and rice to cook. While she was there she would ask the clerk if she bad anything from the western union. "No" the clerk said, "There is nothing today".

"Ok' Maria said, "I am expecting a letter. I will check with you in a few days, maybe next week." "That will be fine" the clerk said. Maria had asked the clerk to get her a sack of beans and a bag of rice. While she was waiting on the clerk to get the order, an older lady came in the door, went over to where the coffee was and picked up a can and stood at the register.

"I'd be with you in just a minute Ms. Lopez "she said "that will be just fine, I'm not in a hurry." Ms. Lopez replied as MS Lopez turned to look at some other items in the store, she turned to the clerk and ask her, "Do you know anybody that does laundry for people that live here in this town."

"No I have not heard of anyone that does that yet that live here." the clerk replied Maria thought to herself, this is my chance to work, so she turned to the lady and said" I do laundry in my home for other people. J would like to give it a try, my name is Maria Sanchez, r live on the west end of town. "Maria says, "That's where I live also, I live close to the river just before the desert" Ms. Lopez replied, "would you like to come over today and we can work out the details on it." "How about one o'clock today "Maria asked.

"Fine" Ms. Lopez says.

As Maria went out the door her heart was happy, she said "I will see you then"

Maria was thinking now of how for so many years that Ms. Lopez had sent her son to school, had bought part of the food that he had eaten. All she could say was to herself, thank you, thank you, only to herself.

Juan had made his way down to the swimming hole with Rio. He knew that he would already be there waiting on him to get there. As he came over the bank of the river it was just as he thought it would be, there was Rio sitting on the rock ledge that was always used as a spring board to jump into the water from.

When Rio saw him he bailed off into the water and yelled to him, "come on in, man I have been here for thirty minutes waiting on you, come on let's get wet. "As Juan was pulling his shorts from over his swim suit, Rio was yelling all the time. Without saying a word he turns and ran as fast as he could go and then yelled "here I come ready or not "almost landing on Rio head.

It was just like any other day at the swimming hole, one ducking the other, yelling and hollering. This went on for almost two hours, then they went and sit on the rock ledge to dry off from their swim. As they sat on the ledge looking across the river Rio looked at Juan and said "do you see anything missing across the river."

"No "Juan replied "what do you mean something missing."

"There is no ranger today singing on the other side." Rio said "you know "replied Juan "J have not seen him today, I wonder where he is at."

"Let's swim across to that thicket and see what it looks like over there. Rio said "1 don't know "Juan replied

"I am going over to see where he is at and see what it looks like over there." Rio said as he gets to his feet and backed up to run and jump as far as he could then swim till he could reach bottom, then they could wade the rest of the way.

Juan says "If you are going I guess I will go to, "as be made his leap off the rock ledge. Both boys was ever looking for someone or for something on the other side. Rio was ahead and he motion for him to head for the thicket that way they could hide in it. They remained very silent, never speaking a word to each other, they just used hand signals.

About the time they were ten feet or so from the other bank the water was only about knee deep, but the rocky bottom was terrible on their bare feet. They were just toeing in the water to not make a sound so if there was someone on the other side of the river bank, they could not hear them. This was their thinking.

As they reached the small thicket that separated the water from the bank, they had to watch for briars, cactus and snakes. They were able to fin d a small path that some animal had made to get-to the water to drink. They were still using hands signals, not speaking a word to each other.

Rio was still ahead as they started up the bank, Juan right on his heels. When they got to the top they were on their hands and knees crawling to get to the top, only to see nothing but desert and the bramble weeds that was everywhere in the desert..

They both stood up about the same time. One looking one way the other looking the other way, neither saw anything that was out of the way, so they breathed sigh of relief. They took a few steps out of the thicket really feeling good about being over in the land of promise.

As they begin to emerge out of the thicket into the desert they began to look ahead to what it would be like to go across it. They could see some mountains in the far distance, but they could not tell how far they were from them.

As they got further out in the desert they could feel the hot sand on their feet as it began burning their toes and on the sole of their feet. They were only about a hundred feet from the levy when they heard a noise of an engine start up. As they looked at each other, a white ranger's truck appear from out of the other side of the thicket that they had just came out of.

Without any hesitation, not even looking at each other, it was to each his own. In other words, run for your lives was the thought of both Juan and Rio. The only reason the ranger could not get to them fast enough, his wheels was spinning in the desert sand, but these boys had good traction and they had it in high gear. The ranger made it to the point that the boys was headed, but when they saw where he went, Rio went to the left and Juan went to the right.

The ranger decided to go after Juan because he had chosen a clear path to the river, but it did not take him long to find out he was no match for the boys and their speed. When Juan was about half way across the river, Rio finally hit the water, but the ranger knew he could not be a match for either of these boys. They were scared, but they were also fast.

Slowly he turns and makes his way back up to the levy to where his truck is parked. He gets in it just to rest for a moment from the ordeal that has just taken place. As he is sitting there he looks across the river and there is the two boys on the big rock ledge. He gives his normal wave to the boys, they grin back and waves back to the ranger.

As the boys are sitting there just looking at the water, not even looking at each other, there is complete silence when Rio finally breaks the silence,

"You know I never could see you until I hit the water. I did not know if he had you or not. When I came out of that thicket I saw you almost across the river, then I knew that you were safe. I knew then we were both ok.

Rio had not even been looking at Juan while he was talking to him, he was still looking at the water. Again Rio looks at Juan and says to him "are you alright." Then Juan looks up at Rio and he had tears in his eyes, he could hardly talk when he fin ally said, 'you know how close we came to being in jail somewhere. I think of how close I came to blowing my field trip, maybe losing my mom forever. How stupid can we get by just playing around?"

"One day Juan we are going to go across and work in the fields." Rio says

"Yes, but today was not the day and it almost cost us everything, let's wait for that day before we do it again"

Juan begin looking at Rio's body, it has scratches all over it from the briars and the cactus he had ran through, Juan could not but to say, "are you sure that you are all right"

"Yea, sure I 'm ok, I will doctor them when I get home.

"Speaking of home, we bad better head that way "Juan says "as they beaded for their bikes, " let's not tell nobody what happened today or I won't be able to come down no more" he continued on.

When he arrives home there sat his mother in the swing under the big cottonwood tree. "How was the swimming today, anything exciting happened" she asked.

No mom it was just an ordinary day at the swimming hole, why do you ask. "Oh I was just wondering, son I need a favor from you if you will do it for me,"

"Sure mom what is it you want done he ask." Will you take the basket of clothes over to Ms. Lopez so they will have them for tomorrow" she replied.

He walks over to the clothes, picks them up and heads down the street to where Ms. Lopez live. When he gets to the house he rings the door bell and she comes to the door and says to Juan, "how is your day going today "as she takes the clothes from him, "anything exciting happening today."

"No, not much going on today" he says pondering all along did they know something that they were not supposed to know. All along thin king to himself, if only her and his mom know what a day it had been.

When he gets back home his mom ask him "when is your field trip coming up, it's only a few day from today isn't it. You had better get together what you are going to take with you. You know that you are staying with a family, so you had better clean up every day, wash before you go to the table to eat. Watch and see what they Jo, and try to practice it.

"Yes mom" he says as he heads I n the house to gather a few things to take with him. She knew that she would have to get together what he needed before it was all said and done. She had been putting back a few dollars for him to take that he don't know about. He can bring back him a souvenir from America.

The letter from school said they would leave on Monday and come back home on Friday. There would be four students going all together. Each one would have a family to live with while they were own the trip.

While in school for the next few days Rio would question him about running away while he was there. He would tell hi, no, he did not want to be a fugitive from his country. He would wait until they bad the chance to go together.

After school was out, when there was nothing going on, not while he was on his trip that he would find or try to find the best way to go and find out from some that had been there and worked there before, but now all that he wanted to do was think about his trip next week.

Maria had everything that she thought that he would need. She had tried time and time again how he was to conduct himself while he was staying with the family.

When Sunday finally rolls around, Juan heads for mass to meet Rio and talk about what will happen when he gets back. He tells him how they would make plans to go over and work before the crops were gone. Juan had asked Rio to find out who that was in town that had been over and worked in the last few years, so when he gets back he could go and talk with him to find the best way to go across the desert.

"Do you want to go swimming today after mass" Rio asked

"No, all l want to do is go home and let the day pass off as fast as it can so I can get a good night sleep tonight so l can stay awake on the bus tomorrow and see the country side. I will see you when I get back.' Juan says as he turns to leave he waves a good bye to him.

How he wishes that Rio would be able to go with him to an America, but he knew that he would not take part in any activities that they held in school. The only reason that he went to school was because his father made him go to get an education so he could find a job in the larger cities.

But now Juan wanted to put today behind him so he could go home and make sure that everything was ready for the bus tomorrow. When he reached home his mom was fixing supper. He walked in to the kitchen then went to the table and sat down and begin to question on what he was taking with him, was it all ready, did he need to go see if she had packed all he wanted to take.

As his mom listened to all of his questions, she knew he would see things in America that he had never seen before. One of the things that she knew he would see was a lawn mower. He had used one of them a couple of times before when the neighbors asked him to mow their Yard. It could not hardly be defined as a lawn here in this part of the country. It had ninety percent weeds and the rest was grass. Grass would not grow because of the lack of rain that they get through the summer months.

Modem technology was not in this part of Mexico yet. T.V was for the elite people, one maybe two stations at the most, and it was all in English language, so they did not understand most of the dialogue.

Maria husband Manuel, Worked in the factories a few years back for a little while to get enough money to put a well down then put running water in the house. It was cold water, yet it beat carrying water from the river. There was no hot water.

When Maria had finished with supper she asked Juan to sit for a while so she could tell him what he might see when he got to where he was going. Most of the things she was going to tell him, he had already heard from some of the people in town that knew he was going, some of them that had already been to America before.

As Juan sat and listened to all his mother had told him, she noticed that his eyes were going closed every now and then so she said, "Juan, You must go to bed now and 1 will wake you in the morning early enough for you to get cleaned up".

Juan still half asleep says "mom make sure you get me up early enough to catch the bus, and I got other things to do before I leave."

"You don't worry about a thing son, 1 will wake you in plenty of time" she replied. Then she starts to clean up the kitchen thinking what a good son that he had turned out to be, and now she did not want anything to happen to him.

She knew that Juan's night would be a fast one because he would not know nothing until morning, but she also knew her night would be a sleepless one thinking about him being gone for a week for the first time being away from her. He would be with people he had never seen before.

Early the next morning as the sky in the east begin to lighten up for the morning, a little bell starts ringing on the alarm clock that Maria had set, so she could get Juan some breakfast before he began his four trip. She let him sleep until she had the meal almost finished, then she made her way to his bedroom to say, "it's time to get up, go wash up for breakfast and then and come and eat.

"Is it time to go, did 1over sleep, Mom what time is it, am I late "he asked in a frantic voice. She knew he was not full awake yet, so she went and put her hands on his shoulders to calm him down from the excitement of being woke up.

Juan you need to wake up and go wash up very good and come and eat." she said "will I have time to do that Mom, will that make me late for the bus "he asked No Juan, you do as I say and you will have plenty of time to catch the bus, "Maria said as she lays his wash cloth and towel out for him, then she goes back and finishes the meal for the two of them. When Juan comes to the table in almost a run, he jerks the chair out from the table and sat down real quick and says, "Mom where is the food. I am going to be late, hurry up mom"

"now Juan you are getting into too big of a hurry, You just slow down and you will be an hour early for the bus anyway, so you just settle down" she says as she finish setting the food on the table, "you just take your time, eat slow so it will digest well. You have a four trip, so take your time. She pointed out to him. But he just could not sit there and eat without looking out for the bus out the door. Then he would walk out the door in the house about every five minutes wondering where the bus was at.

"Juan why don't you just sit down outside so you can see if anybody else is going to the school this early in the morning. If then you see someone go you can go to, or you have to wait until six fifteen, then you can go" she says, "if l wait until that time l may miss the bus mom." he said. "It will take you only ten minutes to get to school, so please sit down for a little while and I will tell you when it is time for you to go. "Maria tells him.

To Juan the next thirty minutes was the slowest that he had ever experienced in his life. Every five minute he would go look at the clock. Then Maria came to the door and said it was about time for him to leave for the school, for him to get all his stuff together. She knew there would be nobody else there, but he could wait there just as could at home. When she said it's time for you to leave he grabs his back pack with all his belongings., it was heavy but to him it was nothing the way he was slinging it around as he headed out the door.

"Wait a minute, wait a minute, what about your poor old mom, don't she get a good by hug and a kiss. "She knew that when she asked for a kiss that was asking a little too much, being be was just like his father in this respect. And yet he planted a big one on her cheek to her surprise. "You are going to be gone from me for a week that's why I need that bug and a kiss." she said.

His feet did not seemed to touch the floor until he had his arms around her waist, and as quickly as he could started to push away, but she held on for a few seconds for the peck on the cheek.

"Mom let me go. ('m going to miss the bus, I will see you when I get back" he says as he ran out the door "oh mom tell Rio to watch my bike at the school for me while I am gone.

"I will see him at mass, or on the street, I will tell him" as she waves good bye to him. Then the tears started coming down her cheek. She could not hardly control herself knowing that for a few days she would be alone all by herself. And she knew it would be this way when Juan decided to go across the river somewhere to work, and if not working, he would be like his dad somewhere out there dead and nobody knows where.

She was hoping that maybe in some way this trip for him would bring him to the idea that he did not need to go across the river to work. That maybe a job in the larger cities would be ok when he saw what it was in America to work for a living. She sat down in her rocking chair on the front porch to ponder all these things. ..

Juan had never peddled his bike this fast down to school before, even when he was in a hurry. As he gets to the school house, there sitting on the steps was Rio. Just like at the swimming hole, always there waiting on him to show up.

"Hi Rio, what are you doing down here this early." Juan asked

"I just wanted to say good bye to all of you, and hope you have a good trip hats all. "He says "Hey I told mom to tell you to watch my bike here for me while I am gone." "Sure will" he said

The boys sat and talked for the next thirty minutes when the bus drives up to pick the kids up. They were all there but one girl that had not showed up yet. The driver told the students that he would wait ten minutes, then he would be pulling out to get on the road. Just about nine minutes had passed and here comes the other student crying like she had been left, she says "My mom let me over sleep, and I did not have nothing to eat." she says

The driver did not seemed to be bothered by the excuses, so he informed them that they were pulling out for the trip. As the bus begin to move, Juan looks out the window and sees Rio running alongside, waving at him so he waved back to say good bye.

A short distance further up the road Maria gets a glimpse of the bus as it is beading out. A bit not comes up in her throat, tears begin to fall on her cheeks again as she is left all alone for a whole week by herself. She would be thinking what kind of family would he be staying with, how would he act in front of them, would he be good.

'All the letter said that she had received from school was that each child would be living with a foster family for a week just to learn what the American culture was, how they lived here, what they ate, how was their leisure time spent.

Maria knew she had raised Juan up to respect his elders, so she was not worried about how he would behave, she was proud he had earned the trip. But now what was going to happen when he returned. Would he forget about going across the river to work? She would have to just wait and see.

Juan had never ridden on a bus before. When he and Maria would go to the city they would usually go with a neighbor who had a car, and then it would be on a one day trip. So now here is Juan with his eyes glued to the windows trying to sake land and what it looked like, but the darkness would not let him see what he wanted to see.

Juan was listening to every word the other students was saying about the families that they hoped they would get. One says she wanted this, the other wanted to see this, each one wanted to see something different, but he just wanted to see some of the fanning ground, he wanted to see if there was any jobs to work at.

About half way to the river check point the sun had broken the horizon enough for Juan to see the desert and the cactus that was all over the land scape, so he just sat back and watched the desert go by, A little over two hours they reached the check point on the river crossing, The driver explained that the children was on a field trip and would be returning the next Saturday morning.

Juan looked outside the bus and he saw men looking at every place on the bus you could hide anything. About that time the border patrol informed the students that he was going to let a dog come on the bus, so they needed to leave their bags and come off the bus for a moment. After they were off, they let the dog come aboard for only a short time then he got off and informed the students they could get back on the bus and told the driver to go ahead on his trip.

When the driver had pulled away from the check point the told the students that they were in America now. They would be to where they were going in little over two hours. He told them to relax and to enjoy the scenery.

Every now and then they would run upon a field of green vegetation, lettuce cabbage, sometimes a patch of com. They had never seen anything as green as these fields were, this was what Juan wanted to see. Sometimes there would be people working in them and he just wanted to be there working also.

The driver told the kids they had about an hour left to go before they arrived at the place to meet their families, so try to have everything ready to get off. Juan just could not keep his eyes off of the farming that was there in the desert.

Before long the driver had slowed down to make a turn to head for the little town of Hundo, a town of about thirty five hundred people. The town had thrived on the farming business that was taken place around it. It had the shipping facilities, it had the storage it needed to keep it until it could be shipped out. It had a river it needed for the homes that was in the town.

The driver now had to make a turn into the school parking lot where a few cars were parked waiting on the children to arrive. They had already been informed by their letters to have their children back here on the school lot next Saturday morning at five o'clock sharp for the return home trip.

As the children got off the bus they were told to line up and their families would call their names so they could go home with them. The name Juan Sanchez was called. A man and a woman approached Juan and introduced themselves. The man said if you want to call us Mr. and Ms. Wilson that will be fine with us.

"By the way son "Mr. Wilson asked "have you ate dinner yet '. "Not since breakfast this morning "Juan replied

"Ok let's go get a sandwich to hold us over until Mary fixes us some supper later on. Then we will go riding around later in the evening and let you see the country side."Mr. Wilson said. Juan just nodded his head as he threw his bags in the back of Mr. Wilson car.

Mary asked "what have you seen that you liked so far."

"The green grass and the fields. How do they get it that green for so Jong" He asked

Mr. Wilson tried to explain to him about the lake and the river that carried water for the fields and for their homes. Juan just sat there and took all that he could he in He finally ask Mr. Wilson what was his job that he worked at. Did he work in the fields or where.

Mr. Wilson tried to explain to him how that they brought the vegetables to a place called a warehouse. There they were stored, packaged, and then shipped from the warehouse. He was the one that ran the warehouse. He told Juan that tomorrow that he would take him down to the warehouse and let him see how the operation worked, but he said today we are going to mow the yard and take care of things around the house first.

"Great" Juan replied

As they pulled onto the yard, Juan noticed how green the yard was. He had never seen nothing like this before. When he gets out of the car he could not but help to put his hands in the grass and feel the blades through his fingers. He sees Mr. Wilson looking at him feeling the grass and he says, "we don't have grass like this where we live, all that grows there is weeds and cactus in Cobos. This is nothing but beautiful.   \.

He continues on to the car to get his bag as Mary sys for him to follow her to his room. Their home was so much different from theirs. It was all painted on the inside and the outside also, be just could not believe how it looked.

Juan changed his clothes and pit on his shorts and sandals to help Mr. Wilson mow the yard. He was already mowing when Juan got outside so Mr. Wilson turns the mower off and instructs him on the safety and the danger of using the mower. Juan told him he had mowed a couple of times with a mower when the neighbors had something else to do he would help them out, so he knew a little about the mower.

Ina few minutes Mr. Wilson looks out and sees Juan cleaning up the mower as if he was done. "Are you finished be asked"?

""Yes' Juan replied. Mr. Wilson went and looked at the front and then went to the back and saw that He had done a wonderful job. The other ones that he hired to do the yard took almost three times the time to get it finished. He looks at Juan and says "that's a faster job than I do, you did a great job. "Thank you sir" again Juan says "let's go eat" Mr. Wilson said, Then we will go to the warehouse and see the workers, but first let me give you something for the job well done" He preceded to hand him a five dollar bill, Juan took it and thanked him for it.

When they had finished their meal he asked Mary if he could help with the dishes but she told him just to go outside and look around until Brandon gets ready to go to the warehouse. He would holler for him when he gets ready to go. He walks outside and he is still amazed how green everything was. The desert had been turned into a green garden.

When Brandon came out to go to the warehouse, as they were riding along he tried to explain how the lake and the river gave them enough water to keep everything green for almost all year until the winter came in the fall for about two months, then they would start all over again in the fields. He needed someone to take the job and keep everything going in the fields year round. They would need a couple years of college courses to learn the ropes.

Juan had l listen carefully what Brandon had said to him, yet he was more interested in the field workers than he was in an office job, he wanted to know how the workers were paid for a day's work in the fields. He told him that the workers drew six dollars and seventy five cents per hour for the first year, then if they were hard workers and stayed on the next year they would receive a raise in their pay.

"Man J need a job like that to help my mother pay her bills when I get out of school" Juan said. He explained to Brandon how that his mother would lose her government check when he graduated from school the coming week.

"*Mr.* Wilson," Juan says "this is my dream to someday come here and get a job here and make a living for my mother where she will not have to work so hard no more."

"We will see if we can work on that and see what we can do about it." Brandon said.

After they arrived at the plant they went through the warehouse and seen the whole operation, then after a awhile Brandon told Juan just to go look around for a while and see the other part of the factory. Juan began to wander around and look and see how the people worked. He talked to a couple of the men and asked them if they ever heard of his dad, telling them his name and what he looked like, but they said they never heard of him.

After spending most of the afternoon at the job site, they went back home. He told them that he was going to his room to rest and call it a day. Before he left the room Mr. Wilson told him that he was going to the warehouse the next morning and he could look at the landscape around the house and the trees and pull all the unwanted grass from around them. He nodded that he would take care of it tomorrow.

Early the next morning Brandon got up early to go to his work. He got dressed so he would not wake anyone up when he went out the door to go to his car, but when he gets outside there was Juan already on his hands and knees pulling grass from among the flowers.

"Son you did not have to do that this early, anytime today, just don't get too hot" he told him" Mary will have breakfast in a little while, she will yell at you then so you be ready."

"Yes sir I will" Juan replied.

He thought that he was taking his time pulling the weeds yet he was done in a short time wanting all the time to down at the warehouse with Mr. Wilson. His mind was on the workers and the jobs that they were doing. After about an hour Mary yelled for Juan to come in for breakfast. He goes to wash up so he can get to the table and see what is for breakfast.

Mary is sitting across from him at the table, and she began to question him about his school, about His mom, and then about his dad. They had sat for about two hours talking about his family and about the life he knew growing up in Mexico. He told her about his father wanting to work in the fields to make a Jiving for his mom. now he wants to do the same thing, and he told her that one day he was going to cross the river at home and come to the states to work in the fields for his mother's sake.

After he told all that he knew about his family he ask her to tell him about the warehouse where Mr. Wilson worked. She started by telling him that the warehouse had been in the family for the last seventy five years, but now none of the family wanted anything to do with running it no more and he did not know what he was going to do with it.

Mary looked at Juan and asked, "do you think you could ever learn to run the warehouse?" "Yes I believe I could with the proper training and work with the field laborers for a while. I think I could learn how to do it." Juan said.

"what would you say if Brandon sent you to college for a couple of years and they would let you get the proper training you needed to see what it would take in the farming part of it. They would teach you how to plant and what to plant for the most profit. We do notjust go out in the field and plant a crop because we like it, we have to do it to make a profit in it to pay our expenses. You would probably would have to work in the fields during the day and go to classes at night. You know if you set your head to it I believe you could do it. We will have to talk to Brandon about it before you leave to go back home. "Mary said.

After they had talked for a while longer he spoke up and said, "I had better go and get those weeds out of the flowers before he gets back home, but before I go back to work I was wondering if after I get done I could go down to that little store that we passed down the street and get me a soda and a bag of peanuts for me to eat on this afternoon.?" he asked

"You sure can, do you think you can find it and make it back home ok?" she asked "do you need any money."

"Oh no ma'am I got money he gave me yesterday from mowing the yard. (will finish my work then I will go down there and get them" "he said Then he went through the whole ordeal about Carlos buying a soda and a bag of peanuts when he came to town with money, and he told her he always wanted one also as he turned and goes out the door to finish his work.

For the next few minutes while she was doing the dishes she would look and see if he bad left yet. After about an hour she noticed he was not in the yard so she thought maybe he was gone to the store so she would watch for him, to come back.

Juan had put all the tools back in place and had headed down the street to the store. His mind was not on the direction that he was going, not paying attention of the turns that he was making to go to the store. He was thinking on trying to run a factory like this in the near future. Finally he reached the store and he went inside.

He was feeling so proud of himself to get to buy him a soda and a bag of peanuts. He handed the Clerk a five dollar bill that he had gotten from Brandon for mowing the yard. The clerk in turned gave him back four dollars and a few cents in change back. He just stuck them in his pocket as he opened the soda and poured the peanuts in the bottle.

As he walked out of the store he was thinking how good that was, when he noticed one large boy and two small one's coming from around the comer of the store. The large boy yelled "hey we want that drink that you have. "Juan replied "well they sell them in the store there."

"We want that one and the money they gave you back so we can buy another one. Juan knew now that he was in for some trouble. As turns to run across the street, he had not noticed the two small boys had come up behind him and so as be turned, each one of them gabbed his arms, then before he had a chance to do anything the large kid hit him in the face. Juan kicks at him, but the boys jerked him back where the big boy was out of reach. Now the boy hit him with two blows in the stomach knocking the breath out of him as he goes to the ground. When he hits the ground they kick him in the stomach adding more pain to his body.

As Juan lay on the ground he see the large boy going through his pocket getting the money he just put there. The money he made from mowing the yard. The money that Maria gave him was put in his back pack and some of it was in his sock. But they were not interested in that money for he was trying to get to his feet all the time.

When he did finally get to his feet be sees that the boys were going in all different directions. As he tries to make out which way they were headed. He could only see out of one of his eyes, the one the boy had hit him in was almost shut now at this time, but he could make out this one boy headed up the street in front of the store, so he started to run after him.

The boy would run through the alleys and dart in the street for a short distance then return back to the alleys again trying to lose Juan. The boy had ran a long ways now making turn after turn trying to lose Juan, and now Juan was in such pain that be had to give up the chase.

Juan made his way back out to the street and looked both ways but he did not have any knowledge of where he was at, he did not know which he needed to go to get back to the Wilson's house or to the warehouse either. For the next hour or so he just walked the streets hoping that he would see one of the boys again, but it never happened.

After a short while he finally ran upon another store, he still had a little money in his sock, so he got to it and went in and bought him another soda and a bag of peanuts to pour into it. Then he tum to the clerk of the store and ask him if he knew where the Brandon Wilson's warehouse was and the clerk told him he did not know where it was, but there was one on up the street where the fanning ground started, so he went down the street to see where it was at, but when he arrived at it, they had all gone home, so he started walking again.

Meanwhile back at the Wilson's house Mary had been watching for Juan to come back home for the last few Hours. She goes out in the yard to make sure that he was not there, that he had not come back and not told her, but she could not find him. She became very scared and thought that she had better call Brandon at the warehouse.

After speaking with the receipts at the desk, she ask to speak to Brandon Wilson that it was an emergency. The lady had to go run him down and told him he had an emergency phone call. When he finally made it to the phone, thinking all along that Juan might have gotten hurt by the lawn mower or something like that, but Mary began telling him about him going to the store a few hours ago and that he had not returned at this time.

When Brandon listen to what Mary had to say he told her that he would run over by the store and see if he could see him and talk to the clerk and see if he knew anything about him. She finally asked "Brandon do you think that he might have ran away and will not come back."

"No I don't think he would do that. He wants to work in the fields to bad" Brandon replied. "Think that he likes it too much here to do something like that. When I go the store and find out what I can I will come borne and we will go riding around to see if we can find him"

Brandon starts driving from the warehouse about the time that Juan gave up on chasing the boy. He drives straight to the store gets out of his ca and looks around for a few minutes then goes inside so he could talk to the clerk.

"Did you see a young Mexican boy about seventeen years old in shorts and a blue tee shirt on and wearing sandals, he should have been here about one or two o'clock this afternoon." Brandon asked the clerk thought for a moment and said "yes r remember him, he got a soda pop and a bag of peanuts, then left". "Do you know which way he might have gone when he left. "He asked

"No I don't know where he went, but I did hear noise and stuck my head out the back door and seen three boys fighting with him. Two was holding him and one was hitting him very hard" the clerk said, "but which way they went I do not know."

Thanks Brandon says to him as he goes out of the store to go get Mary to start driving around. It has begun to get a Little dark by now. Juan was not afraid of the dark, but to be in a strange place and it began to get dark was a weird feeling, he had come to the realization now that he was lost and did not know which way to go to find home.

His body was beginning to ache with pain that he had never known before, pain from the blows to his face was hurting the most. His eye is completely shut now. It's getting darker and darker now he comes to a park like setting with a few benches in it. Some of the seats was behind bushes so you could sit and look over the waters of the small pond. So he sat down for a little and tried to gather his thoughts together, but before he knew it he had laid his head down and he had fell fast asleep.

Brandon had went and picked up Mary and they started to driving up one street and down the other until it was too dark for them to see any longer, so he decided to go to the police station and see if they had heard of someone being in a fight. He walks into the station to find two deputies playing cards. He relates the story to them of why he was there, and what he had done, and the three boys attacking Juan at the grocery store. \.

After talking with the officers for a few minutes he left the station and went to his car and just sit there for a few moments when Mary asked, "what is wrong Brandon? "Well I did not tell you what the clerk told me about him being in a fight when three boys attacked him in front of the store. Why they did we do not know at this time, we do not know how bad he is hurt. We won't know this until we find him and see if he is hurt, so now let's go home and let the police try to find him for us.

Mary became frantic when she heard that he had been in a fight after being attacked. She looked at Brandon and asked, "Do you think we ought to check with some doctor office somewhere."

"No "be replied "he did not know where a doctor office was in this town. Let's just go home and wait on the police to do their job, see if they can find out anything on their patrol. "The night passed off very slow for them. They had stayed up way past their bed time but nobody had called them so they went on to bed.

The next morning Brandon gets in his car and goes on down to the warehouse to tell his office that he would be gone for a while and then he left to go searching again. All the time that morning he looked for Juan, he was on the wrong end of town to where Juan was.

Juan in the meantime had been on the move since early dawn. He had remembered the money that his mother had given to him. Some of it he had put in his backpack and the rest he had put in his sock. He sat down and takes out about two dollars so when he runs upon another store he can buy him a cake and soda. This time he remembers what happen just a few hours before.

He makes his way down the street and finds another comer store. He goes in and find a soda and a cake and then ask the clerk, "sir do you know where Mr. Wilson bas a warehouse at. He has all kinds of vegetables there that he ships to other parts of the country."

"No" The clerk says "there is three or four warehouses around the town, but l do not know the name of any of them, sorry, are you all right, do J need to get you some one to help you."

"No I'm alright I just need to find the warehouse that Mr. Wilson owns, thank you anyway "Juan replied. While Juan was talking to the clerk, Mr. Wilson went by the store, and on the other side of the highway the police patrol went by also still looking for Juan. As Juan comes out of the store he is trying to figure which way to go, what direction to take, so he just start walking again. He had been walking for about three hours when a patrol car pulls up beside him and start talking to him. They ask him all kinds of questions, finally one of the officers said, I heard the night patrol officer mention a Mexican boy being lost that had been in a fight, so he looks at Juan and see that his face is still black and blue, his eye is completely shut now, so he ask Juan, "Where do you live"

Juan replied, "L am staying with Mr. Wilson, he runs a big warehouse where all the produce is, l don't know his address.

"Come on let's find the Wilson warehouse and try to get this settled. "The officer said. On the way to the place Juan explains what had happened to him at the grocery store. When they arrive and pulls into the yard, Brandon pulls in from the other side of the parking Jot and see the officer's car and heads for it to see if they have found out anything. As he pulls up and gets out of his car, the door on the patrol car opens and Juan leaps out and goes to Brandon and gives him a big hug and a large smile. "I'm sure glad to see you Mr. Wilson."

"I am glad to see you too, let's sit over at the break table and you tell me and the officers what happened "Brandon say's So Juan relates from the time he left the yard from pulling weeds, until the officers picked him up about an hour or so ago. Then the police questioned Juan about the size and the looks of the boys. They explained to him, they just wanted to be on the lookout for them if they might see someone that look like them.

As the officers left Brandon looks at Juan and say's "do you want to go to the doctor?"

"No I'm ok l probably need to go out in the field and work this afternoon.'

"No you are going home and rest for the rest of the day and let Mary see you. She is worried to death about what happened to you. And when I get home this afternoon we will go riding around so you can see what some of the other country looks like. You can see some of the other fanning ground, if the will be ok with you, but first you go home and get some rest and take a nap if you want to. "Brandon says," That was the thing he wanted to hear Brandon say, that was what he came to see, that was the farming ground and the opportunity that it had for the workers. He wanted to see how they harvested the crops, he wanted to know where the crops went to when it was shipped out.

When he arrives at home, Mary could not believe how he looked, all beat up. The bruises was turning all different colors now, the eye was really black by now, and the bruises on his stomach was really showing up now. Mary wanted to doctor them but he just wanted to go take a good hot shower and lay down for a short nap.

He goes to his room, Brandon goes back to the warehouse to finish the day there. After Juan gets up from his nap, he noticed that he had slept a little longer than he was wanting to. He opened his door only to smell food cooking in the kitchen so he hurried into the kitchen to find Mary just about to finish up with supper, and there was Brandon driving up in the driveway.

As he comes into the house by the way of the back door, he gives Mary a kiss on the cheek, say's hello to Juan and ask him how his evening went, he tells him ok, and he only slept to long.

Mr. Wilson sat down at the table and Juan follows him as he grabs his chair and begin waiting on himself. Brandon ask him if he was hungry, he told him yes because he had not eaten since this morning when he got that soda and a cake. During the meal< Mary wanted to know all about the boys that robbed him, so he told her all he knew about them.

When he had finished his supper Juan jumps up and starts to cleaning up the dishes when Mary tells him to leave them, that she would do them while Brandon would take him riding in the country side.

"Come on Juan, let's go for a ride in the outskirts of the country. We will see what other farmers grow, and how they handle it. As they drove for mile after mile, Juan sat and marveled at the work to be done. He would ask a question before Brandon had time to answer it he would ask another one. He just could not get over the questions that he was asking about the workers.

Finally Brandon ask him "How would you like to someday to come here and take over the whole operation. You would have to go to college for a few years, then you could work in the fields during the day and learn that part of it. In college they would teach you what you would have to plant to get the best return for your money. While you are working I n the field that would pay your schooling."

"Mr. Wilson that would be the dream of my life to come here just to work in your fields, but to try to learn all of it, that would be awesome, but sir I could do it if you want me to. "Juan answered "But I have never had a chance to do something like this in my whole life. I could support my mother and she would never have to work again." "Well maybe we could change that someday, where your mother would not have to work no more. It is going to take time, but we will work on it to get you back over here."Mr. Wilson said. In the back of Juan's mind it may not be as long as he thinks, for before long he was going to come back to work in the fields on his own with Rio.

When they arrive at home and go in, Mary tells them to sit at the table to eat a peach cobbler that she made while they were gone. As they were sitting around the table Mr. Wilson ask Juan, "you only have two days left here with us, those two days belong to you, what would you like to see, or maybe what would you like to do."

"Sir, if you would let me do it, I would like to work in the field to see what it is like, that is my dream to someday come here and work every day in your field."

"That is the only thing you want to do is just to work every day, but you have an opportunity to go and see other things while you are here." He said, "I will see them while I am here all the time, now I want to see the working part of it to see if I can do it or not." Juan replied.

"Well you be ready in the morning and make sure that you grab a straw hat on the way out for that sun gets real hot in the fields. They are behind the washer hanging up on the wall and you be ready when I leave to go to the warehouse." Brandon said.

Jumping to his feet he says "I'll be ready when you are sir, thank you very much. "Then he heads for his bedroom to get a good night sleep. Brandon watches him as he heads for his room then remarks to Mary what must be in a boy to want to work instead of going looking around at the places to see? He remarked that it seem like that he was possessed with wanting to work. He told Mary about him talking to him about going to school and maybe someday run the operation for them. He said that would be wonderful

For the next two days Brandon would watch Juan work. Then he would talk to the other workers about what kind of worker he was. They said he was never behind in his work, he would even help those that got behind, help them catch up. It seemed that his energy was never depleted from his body.

When Brandon would go home at night he would tell Mary how that the boy would work right along with the rest of the crew, how that he would make sure that everything was put up for the day before he left the place for the night. May told Brandon how that she also had talked to him about him coming and seeing after the operation when he had finished his college to learn the financial part of it.

Brandon then said, "It will take me awhile to get a working visa for him but l think it would be worth the effort if I could do it. It would be worth us enrolling him in the college for the two year course. "Mr. Wilson said, "but tomorrow he will go back to his home land, to a land of, as he calls it, the land of nothing."

The next morning bright and early they went in and woke Juan for breakfast to get him ready to catch his bus back to his home country. As they sat around the table talking, Mr. Wilson tried to explain his plan to try to get him to come back for a longer stay the next. He told him it was going to take a while for him to get everything.

All the time that Brandon was explaining the plan, Juan was thinking that he would be back here in a few weeks by his own self, him and Rio.

It was time to leave for the school to catch the bus. When they arrived at the school, the bus was already there, and as always Juan was the first one there. When they get out of the car Mr. Wilson ask Juan for his back pack to put an envelope in it and for him to tell his mother about it and for him to give it to her when he gets there.

Finally at the appointed time all the children was there except for the same girl that was late when they left Mexico to come here. The driver made the comment that he could not leave her over here, because he would have to come back and get her by his and he did not want to wait on her again.

After about ten minutes here comes the girl crying that no one woke her up, she had missed her breakfast, to which the driver said to her, let's go, we have heard this before. The trip going home was no longer going than it was coming back home, yet to them it seemed to have taken a longer time to come back than it did to go., but finally they could see the out skirts of this small town, now they knew that the school was not far away.

As the driver made the tum into the drive way there was Rio running alongside of the bus, reaching up and touching the windows every chance he got. As the bus comes to a stop, Juan sits and waits for the girls to get their belongings together before he started to get off the bus, As he steps off Rio reaches and grabs him with a big hug, then looks up at his face and see his black eye and the other bruises that he had, " m a n what happened to you, what kind of a fight were you in, did you win, did it hurt." Rio asked "Look I will tell you all about it after mass tomorrow, but now l need to get home and see mom now, J have some papers to give her from Mr. Wilson," Juan replied "oh. By the way, thanks for looking after my bike", as he waves a good bye to him.

A few blocks away there is a lone figure looking toward the main street that her road connected to. When she sees a bicycle turn the comer, tears start streaming down her face as she opens the door to go out when the bicycle comes to a stop.

Juan comes to his mom, he opens his back pack, then she looks at his face and says, "son what happened to you, how come you to get into a fight," "I will tell you later, Mr. and Ms. Wilson sent you a letter to read. I am supposed to give it to you to read as soon as I get here. "He says as Maria begin wiping the tears from her eyes so she could read what the note said, she could just barely make out the money that was in the envelope. He explained to her it was for the two days' work that he did while he was there. Then he goes into detail about the face of Juan and how it had happened, that it was not his fault, he just tried to protect his self. The note went on and told how that they were going to try to get him a work vise to come back and try to learn how to run the operation, he tried to tell her it was going to take time for them not to give up.

When she finished reading the letter she asked him if he knew about the money, he said no be was just working to help them out. She told him there was about six month of the amount she drew from the government.

He then turns to his mom and says, "Mom I am going to go back and work because he may never get me that visa to go to work. He said it would take a long time, mom we can't wait that long. Soon your check will be cut by the government and then we will not have enough to get by, that is the reason that I am going to go and work while I can. "But son I keep telling you that we will make it some way" she says "We will see mom, we will see' Juan replied She knew back in her heart that the trip did not change his mind about going across the river, and she knew that there was no way for her to stop him from doing that. "Mom you know that I get my certificate from school this coming week, after that our money will be cut out in a few weeks and then what will we do. I know what, we will go to the big city with the other thugs and the slave drivers, Mom we do not need to do that "Juan says "son, let's check and see if there is people going to the city in a few days, maybe for the weekend. With your education now you should be able to get a good job at some factory, or maybe. There is a lot of possibilities when you get out of school. We will have to just wait and see. "Maria says "Come on son, let me fix you a bite to eat then we can talk a little more of us finding a job.

While she was fixing something for Juan to eat, be told her about all that had happened to him while he was on the field trip, about the boys robbing him, beating him up, and the police finding him the next day, about Mr. Wilson wanting to hire him when he gets him a visa to come to Work, but he says mom I cannot wait that long, it may never happen.

After he gets through eating he gets up from the table and goes toward the river where he spent most of the day just looking toward the other side. He knew now what was son the other side and he wanted it more than ever now. He could hardly hold himself from going over to Rio's to find out who they could talk to about what to expect when they tried to cross to the farming ground.

The day passed off at a slow pace for him, but finally it got dark enough to go in and talk to his mother of the things she wanted to know, all about the Wilsons, their life style, things that they ate, and what else she could think of to ask him. Finally Juan said, "mom it's getting late l need to go to bed so I can go to mass tomorrow morning," as he turns to go to his bed room. Maria set for a long time wondering when this one would leave and never come back like the other one did. She knew it was coming, but just did not know when as of yet. Early the next morning before Maria was ready to get up, Juan had fixed him a bowl of cereal and was on his way to see Rio at the church building. He just knew that he would be early enough to beat him there this time, but when he arrived, there he was sitting in front of one of the fountains in the front yard waiting on him. They grabbed each other like they had not seen each other in years.

Well what happened to you, was you in a fight." he asked. Juan bad to tell him all about the fight and everything that had happened to him for the whole week.

"Boy I wish I could have been there, we could have whipped all three of them with ease. They would have been the ones that would have been running for their lives, When we get over there we will go and find these kids and show how we can fight" Rio says "well anyway that is all in the past now, I may not never see these boys again," he replied. "You mean you are not planning on going over there and work now. Man I have been making all kinds of plans to go over. "Rio says "Did you find out who we could talk to about making the trip. They would know what we would need to take with us to get across, maybe they could tell us how long it would take for us to get across." Juan replied.

"Everyone that that I talked to" Rio says. "They told me that a man by the name of Wilson Cruz is the one that we need to talk to He has even gone over and worked for a while back in the early days. Maybe he could tell us about your dad and the men that went with him."

"Why don't you set up a time after school one day for you and me to go talk to him if he will agree to it? He may not want to talk to us, but find out if he will. "Juan said

About that time the bell said it was time for the services to begin, Rio just motioned with his head that he would find out. After the services was over the two boys headed for the door and Rio reached it first, and turns and yells back at Juan. "Do you want to go swimming today, It won't be too long that it will be to cool to go you know"

"No not today, I want to spend some time with my mom, just in case T am not here for very much longer" he slid.

"Ok then" Rio says, "I will go talk to Mr. Cruz about when we can come and see him, Even if he will let us come."

They waved at each other then went on their way. Juan thought he had better spend some time with his mom because he could leave like his dad, Manuel did and never come back home, he did not want that to happen to him like that. All afternoon he stayed at the house the house helping Maria with things she was doing. He volunteered to take the laundry over to Ms. Lopez house, something he only did when he was asked to do. From all that he was doing Maria knew that there was something coming up before long. She knew that it would be just like her husband, he never said a thing about the time or the day that they was going to leave, and now the same with Juan.

She knew that they would be leaving by night because they had to get to some shade by morning.

Maria had never thought to look at the calendar to see when there was going to be a full moon to travel by, then she would have knew about what day it would be they would leave. But now with her mother instinct she knew he was staying close by for some reason, and she had to watch for those reasons to start forming into something else.

The next morning Maria had breakfast ready when she went and awoke Juan to come to eat before going off to school. There was only three days of school left before he was getting out, it would be out for always for him. That what was bothering him.

He could hardly wait to get to school top see what Rio had found out at Mr. Cruz the day before. So right after he finished his meal, he jumped from the table and grabbed his back pack and headed for school as fast as he could ride his bicycle. When he arrived there Rio was sitting there waiting for him to get there.

"What did you find out yesterday "Juan asked?

"Any time man, anytime he said would be alright, he was there most of the time, and he would be sitting under the old white oak tree." Rio said "He asked if we could come over tomorrow evening after we get out of school and I said we will be there, was that ok?"

"Yea that was just fine" he said, "Soon as school is out we will head over there." He was wondering how he would tell his mom that he was going to be late coming home from school tomorrow. He thought that he would tell her something was happening at school and he stayed for it and he hoped she would believe him.

Right after school the next day they headed for Mr. Cruz house. When they arrived there he sat under the big old tree like he said. He knew why the boys were there yet he asked "What can l do for you boys today."

The boys came right to the point of why they were there, "we want to go across the river and work for a while and we need to know what we need to take to survive the trip, when do we leave and things like that." Juan said "In the first place, why did l ask you to come today, not next week, do either of you know why?" he asked. They looked at each other and shook their heads because they did not know why he wanted this week.

Next Tuesday there will be a full moon that is the only one that will be for a while, and that is the only time you can possibly travel through the desert at night, and that is on a full moon. You can see what is ahead and you can see the rattlesnakes that are crawling everywhere.

As far as what you take, you cannot take enough water, you have to find cactus and chew on them to get moisture from them to save on your water to make it last as long as it will. You need two good lights with three sets of batteries for each one of them, and you hope that they will last. You will need long pants, a pair of good boots, you won't make it otherwise, the sand will blister your feet even through your boots in the heat of the desert.

If you do not go this Tuesday night then the next time will be a little over a month later when the moon will be in the next phase and will be light enough for you to see. But let me tell you this, if you decide to leave this Tuesday let me wish you the best of luck for you are going to need it.

The boys talked a little longer and then they started to leave and they thanked Mr. Cruz for the time he took with them and told them what they needed to know. Then they headed for Juan's house where they sat under the white oak tree and talked for a long time about what each one of them would have to get so they would be on the same page.

Without their knowledge Maria had been working in the kitchen and had seen the boys come up the street and sat under the tree and talk for a long time. It only brought back memories of the day that her husband and the other men sat and talked under the same tree twelve years ago. She remembered how that they never returned.

When Rio left Juan went into the house. As soon as he came in the door Maria spoke up, "You boys planning a big swimming party or something this week in I saw both of you having a long conversation with each other.

"No mom we were just talking between ourselves about some things that Rio is doing and he will need some help with before long." Juan says

"Son you need to get ready for supper, it will be ready in a few minutes" she said "You know that tomorrow is the last day of school for you and we need to sat down and talk about what we are going to do before long because you know that the government money will run out before long and we will have to be looking for work before long. I am going to have to put some of the money that Mr. Wilson paid you when you worked for him so that we can have enough to stay overnight when we go to the city to look for work.Juan had a little money he had also put back when he went on the field trip that Maria knew nothing about, but he was going to buy his flashlight batteries and the fruit with it that he needed to take. But before she could say anything else he turned and headed for his bedroom so he would not have to listen to the talk o0f going to the city.

The next morning it was off to school, for this was the day that Juan had been waiting for. He thought that he would be a free person after today. The last day of school was for the most of the students would be the last time they could see a class room because they could not afford to go to college nowhere, all they would have would be the certificate, so now they all wait for the lunch bell to ring and then they would go home.

The two boys on the other hand had other plans. They headed over to Mr. Cruz to see if he had thought of anything else that they needed to know. When they arrived over to his house, there he was under his big tree in the shade as if to be waiting on the boys, beside him he had two canteens for water and an old pair of boots that he told the boys that they could have because he needed them no more. So now all the boys needed was the fruit to eat on and the flashlight batteries. Juan would pick them up later.

All Maria could do was the same thi9ng that she did when her husband wanted to leave back twelve years ago. She knew that the more she talked against it to the boy they would still go anyway. Now she knew it was Juan's turn to go and all she could do was to hope it would have a better outcome she wanted her son to come home safely if he did not get over to work.

The next few days passed off very quickly for the boys as they were gathering up the equipment that they were taking with them. They were making sure that everything was in their backpack that all their clothes was at Rio's house. His dad did not know that anything was going on with the boys, he never paid no attention of them going out or coming in.

Finally the day that they had been waiting on was here, Juan stayed around the house almost all the day helping his mom with all that she was doing. She knew like before that the time was close for them to go across the river and yet all she could do was pray for their safety. The day had passed off real smoothly, the sun was almost ready to set in the west then he tells his mom,

"Mom I am going over to Rio's house to help him with some of his work. I will probably be gone for a little while so don't worry about me. "he says"

As he gets on his bike he turns to say something to his mom, but the words just would not come out as he peddled away. She stood there and watched him leave and then the tears came streaming down her cheeks for she knew that the time was now

As he rides slowly on his bike over to Rio's, he noticed in the eastern sky that there was a big harvest moon just beginning to come up over the mountain rang in the far distance. This was going to be the night that they were to go across the river into the desert.

Mr. Cruz had told the boys to wear shorts when they went to wade the river, then fully dress after you wade the river so your clothes will not hold the sand like they would if they were wet. They had made sure that they had followed his instructions to the letter.

They were fully dressed now and about a quarter of a mile from the river out in the desert. They were in a half walk to a half run, they wanted to save all their energy that they could. They could feel the heat from the sand on their feet already from the heat of the day, but they knew that it would get cooler the further they went into the night.

When they were about two miles out in the desert they heard the lookout overhead and they were still not burning their lights yet. They were looking for some good bushes to run under if they came to close.

Juan yelled to Rio "make sure that you keep your light off when they get close, and when you see their lights you hit the sand under those bushes."

"Don't you think that we better get down until it passes by now" Rio yelled as he dives under a large bush. The lights were running from right to left. It came very close to them but then it turned the other direction and went on their way. They jumped to their feet and continued on through the night. In about another three hours the copter was overhead again. The boys did the same thing that they had done before. It only lasted for a few moments and the boys were on their feet running again.

The closer the grove got to them it seemed the faster they traveled. They knew that when they reached it they could sat and rest for a while. They had traveled till they were about within a quarter of a mile from the grove they heard the lookout copter coming back after only a short time away from them. They knew that they had to get there so they could get some rest. In break neck speed they took off running as fast as they could, but when the copter got almost to them it turned and went another route as if they saw something somewhere else.

When the boys decided to sat for a spell they took some of their fruit and started to chew on it for the nourishment that they needed for their bodies. They rested only for a short time when they decided to continue on their way around the grove. Every now and then they would hear a rattlesnake in the edge of the grove.They had traveled only a short distance around the grove when all of a sudden there was the chopper almost overhead. This time they were going around the edge of the grove to see if they could see anything at the edge. Rio yelled "" Hey this looks like a good path, let's get out of his way so they won't see us." As he made a dash into the thicket with Juan right behind him. He tells Rio to keep his light off for a little while till the lookout goes on their way.

In a short while all was clear when Rio turned his light on when Juan says Don't go to deep in the grove, you remember what Mr. Cruz told us about the snakes" He had no more than said that when Rio let out a scream' Come here, hurry, some here." Thinking that he had been snake bit Juan runs like a deer would run. When he gets to Rio there he stands with his light on a full skeleton laying on the ground. Juan could think only of his father. He begins to look it over to see if it had any identification on it but it did not.

As he was looking it over he had not noticed that Rio had ventured further into the grove, then he yells again, "come over here, here is another one over here" but as Juan turns to go there, Rio yelled again "I am bitten on the hand by a rattlesnake don't come over here, there may be another one" then he heads Towards Juan.

Juan looks at the bite and he tells him "we will have to go back and try to get you home to a doctor or you will die like these that are laying here. Let's make our way out to the edge of the thicket and we will leave ever thing but the water and the fruit we can make better time this way.

Rio says "it will be daylight soon and it will be too hot for us to travel. I am already getting sick, my arm is beginning to burn.

"You come on, let us get out of here back in the edge of the desert" Juan said

As soon as they reached the edge of the thicket Juan started to stripping everything that he thought that they would not need on the way back. He knew that he was going to have to carry Rio All the way back and he wanted it to be as light as possible. Rio was light in stature weighing on a hundred pounds or less. Juan knew it was going to be a struggle but he thought he could do it. He was going to try. He takes a thin sheet which they had to lay on for sleeping and threw it over the body of Rio and headed out in the desert

The sun was a couple of hours from coming up, he knew he would have that much of a head start before the sand got unbearable to walk in. He knew he was going to have to try anyway. About three hours out from the grove the helicopter was flying off in the distance, he did not know if they saw him or not, he did not care he was not going to stop for any reason, unless the heat made him. Every now and then he would stop and put water over the head of Rio to keep him from drying out in the face.

The further he went with the sun up now it is h beginning to have effect on his feet, but he knew that he had to keep going in spite of how he felt. When he was about two hours from the river he thought about giving up, just lay Rio down on the sand and let the heat take its course on both of them, but when he took a look toward the river, he thought that he could make out a figure of a man in the far distance. He did not know if it was real or a mirage that he had heard about all o0f his life. All that Juan knew was that he was going to try to reach that person or die trying.

The distance between the two finally closed up to where he could that it was a man. It was the ranger that sat on the bank of the river all of the time at home, The chopper had notified him that someone was in trouble out in the desert, and the only way that he could help them was to go on foot. The sand would not let a two wheel vehicle go nowhere when they were face to face, Juan tried to talk to him but his mouth was so dry that no words would come out. "You put him on my shoulders and you come behind me. Let us get going before we finally cook out here." The ranger said.

Juan did not know what else to do but what the ranger had told him to do. He could not hold the pace that the ranger was going, he would stop every now and then and take a sip of water, then would have to almost run to catch up. Now the hot sun was almost straight over head. In another hour or so it would be too unbearable to walk in, the ranger knew this. The ranger stop for a moment and told Juan to pour water over his head and the head of Rio to keep the temperature down for a little while, then he was on his way again.

They could see the river now in the distance and Juan begin to wonder what was going to happen when they got to it. Would he load them both in the truck and take them to jail. Was Rio alive or was he dead, what was the ranger going to do with them. About the time they were within a hundred yards of the river the Rangers turns to Juan and asks, "Where did you boys cross the river at." Juan told him it was about two hundred yards up stream, it was a lot shallower there.

Juan was able to run ahead a little now knowing that the ranger was not going to, take them to jail right now. As he cut into the path that they crossed at when they left. On the other bank there was a crowd that had gathered to see what was going on.

Again the ranger says "tell someone to go get a Dr. Quick then you show me where he lives at."

"We are only about two blocks over to where he lives, that's his father over there on the bank, the one standing on the end."

"Tell him to go fix a bed to lay him on when we get there." The ranger said

No sooner than it was said than Mr. Diaz ran to the house and put clean linens on the bed to lay Rio on. By the time he had the bed fixed the ranger came through the door and was taking Rio off of his shoulder so he could lay him on the bed. Then he asked the ranger "is he dead, this is my son"

"No I don't think he is dead but he is very sick, If you will tell everybody to leave the room so the doctor can come in and take care of him. Then when we find out how he is we will let them know" the ranger said, then he turned to Juan and said, "son where do you live, let me take you there so your parents will know that you are all right."

"Yes sir" Juan said "It isn't but a few blocks over on the other road down by the river."

"When the doctor arrives here, then we will go over to your house and see your parents and let them know that you are safe and back at home" he replied. About that time the doctor came into the house and brought some serum for snakebites because he thought that might be the problem.

The ranger explained to the doctor about him being out in the heat, then about being bitten by the snake, then he motioned to Juan to come on and they would go to his house. Juan knew that his mother had not slept since he left last night.

When they got to the house the ranger knocked on the front door, Juan was standing behind the ranger so when Maria aw the ranger she could not see Juan to. Before he could tell her that he had brought Juan home, her knees begin to buckle under and as she started to fall he grabbed her and held her up and said to her, "I have brought your boy home this time, but it may not be this good the next time. They may not come back home the next time"

By now Juan had stepped from behind the ranger, she turned the ranger lose and grabbed hold of Juan and begin to cry then she said to the ranger, "come in and tell me what has happened, is Rio ok, where is he'.

"look ma'am I am going back across the river to let my bosses know where I am at and what has happened also, Your son will tell you all about it, and son when you find about your buddy in the next day or two come and let me know how he is."

"I will sir, I will be there before long and let you know, thank you for everything", He said as the ranger heads for the river to cross over to, his truck.

Maria was all too happy that her son was home safe and sound, but she could not but help herself to say, "You know son, after you took that field trip a few days ago I thought maybe that you would not want to risk your life and try to go back over there for what was there."

"Mom what is over there is worth risking your life for. Over there you do not have to live like we do here. Someday I will be there or I will be like those bodies that we saw in the grove before Rio got bit by the snake. You know mom, probably one of those bodies was dads, but I did not have time to look for identification on either one of them.

All the time they were talking he was pulling off his boots and telling all that had happened. Maria looked down at his feet and saw that they were all blistered so she ran and got a pan of warm water and put salt and alum in it to soak his feet in then she told him to keep them off of the floor till the doctor had looked at them.

Juan tried to explain to his mom about Rio, then he told her that he did not know if he was going to live or to die. Then he told her about the ranger carrying him for the last two or three hours in the desert, and then added that he thought he would have died if he had not did this. They sat and talked for a little while longer then Maria told him that she was going over to see how Rio was then when she got back that she would fix him something to eat. He knew that he was supposed to keep his feet up off the floor until the doctor looked at them.

All the time that his mom was gone he had taken his feet out of the soaking and held them in the air to dry off. She was not gone only for a short time when she came back she brought the doctor back with her so he could examine his feet also. He then gave Maria some salve to put on them to help with the healing. But Juan was more interested in what was happening with Rio. He could not help but to ask the Doctor is he going to die doctor, what is he doing."

'No son, he is a long way from being dead or dying for that matter. He must to have seen the snake just before he struck him and was moving his hand, causing the snake to give him only a glancing blow on the back of his hand by striking the bone and just going under the top layer of skin on his hand and just gave him enough venom to make him deathly sick. He is coming around alright now, he will be ok in a day or two then he looked at Maria and tells her to check with her in a few days if those feet were not better." Which she said she would.

As soon as the doctor had left Juan leaned back in the chair and in just a few moments he was fast asleep. His mouth had begun to blister so she put some of the salve on it also to help with the healing. She was going to let him sleep for an hour or so before she awoke him, but the smell of cooking food could not keep him asleep any longer.

As he straighten up in his chair he began to feel the pain from the sun and from the weight that he had carried across the desert. While he was still in the chair he told Maria about seeing the bodies in the grove, but like before he told her he did not have time to see who they were, then he told her he believed that one of them might have been his dad.

"Well son we will probably never know who those men were, we will never see them again I hope. She said

"But Mom one day I will try again before I go to the large cities to work" he said

"but son you know that you cannot make it across, you know what is out there now." She replied.

"Mom I know what is on the other side and it is worth dying for if you can get there. He said. Maria knew it was no use arguing with him so she began to put food on the table and got him to the table to eat. The next couple of days Juan would only put his feet on the floor for a short period of time.

He knew it was going to take time for them to heal. Then on the third day he had walked to the outside of the house to be in the sun. While he was sitting there, he noticed a figure coming down the road, he could not believe his eyes, it was Rio.

They grabbed each other in a large embrace. Juan told him to grab a chair and sat down for a while and they would talk. Juan began by telling him how the ranger had carried him for the last two or three miles to the river. Rio could hardly believe that the ranger did this for them. Then Rio looked at Juan and said, "I believe that this will be my last trip across the desert."

"Not me" Juan said "I am going to try one more time, I believe I can do it."

"Man you have to be crazy. You know what is out there and you need to leave it alone" Rio says

"We will see" Juan says Then he looked at Rio's hands and seen how that they had turned black and blue and a few other colors, he asked him about it but he told Juan that the doctor told him that the color would go away in time then he would know that all would be ok.

They sat and talked for a couple of hours about their trip, and then Rio left and went back toward his house leaving Juan to think about going across the desert by his self all alone.

In the next couple of weeks he would go and talk to Mr. Cruz about by his self, but he would not even talk to him about making the trip by his self, but he knew that Juan's mind was made up, He was going to try again very soon.

The following Sunday the boy's meet at mass. There they talked about going swimming that afternoon because it had warmed up very good. They said to each other that they would meet after dinner and Juan had a chance to tell his mom where he was going to be at. They had been swimming for about a half hour when they noticed the white pickup sitting across the river almost hid by the weeds as always. When they saw it they both swam to the other side of the river to see if it was the ranger. It was him and he saw them coming so he gets out and waits on them to get there.

Juan spoke first. "Mr. Ranger this is Rio, this is the one we carried across the desert.

"How are you doing son from the bite you got," the ranger asked

" I am doing just fine now, still a little black and blue, but the doctor said it would be back to normal before long." Rio replied.

"You know son, we almost lost you this time' he said "I hope you both will think about it twice the next time you try something like this, even if you make it across you won't be in any shape to work for no body."

Juan spoke again, "I will have to try it again someday, I want to work in those fields on the other side of that grove."

"Son you need to take this old fools advice and don't try it, especially if you are going to try it alone it will not work, don't do it" he said as he opens the truck door and gets back in the truck. The boys turn and go back to the swimming hole and continue swimming for a short while before the quit for the day.

The following week Juan was back over to see Mr. Cruz about the time it would be to go again. Again he was very careful about telling him what day, but he saw that he was bound and determined to go again so he told him that it would be about two weeks on a Thursday night the moon would be in the next phase. Maria knew that he had his mind made up to go again, so she started to watch every move that he made and then she would talk to him about every chance that she got trying to talk him out of it. About twice a week she would go to the store that had the western union in it to see if anything from Mr. Wilson had come for them, but each time she was told nothing had come for them.

Juan had pleaded with Rio to go with him again just this one more time, but Rio told him that he and his father was moving to the big city and find work there. This was a blow to Juan as now he felt that there was nothing going to hold him here. He felt that he was just left all alone in the world. He knew that now there was not no one going to go with him across the desert but his own self.

The week he was going to leave he started to gathering up what he needed to make the trip. Maria kept watching every day, and when she would have the opportunity she would ask him about Mr. Wilson that he should wait for a respond from him but all Juan would say was, you know that is not ever going to happen. It just seem that there was no communicating with him what so ever. His mind was set.

On Monday Maria had noticed that the bag was full and that it was about ready to go. She had to make a trip to the little store to get some rice for their food for the coming week. While she was there she ask the clerk if there was any mail for her, but the answer was the same one as always. She was beginning to have the same feeling that Juan had about Mr. Wilson sending for him.

The week passed off slow for her as she kept watch on the bag in his room. Each day it would get a little fuller to the point that she did not think that he could carry all of it. On Wednesday he had everything that he wanted to take with him in the bag. The next day was the day he was going to leave.

The next day she got to looking for Juan but could not find him, so she ran and looked in his room to see if his bag was gone, but it was still there. As she begin to do her laundry she noticed that she needed detergent from the store so she left the house and went to the store to pick up her detergent and like always she started to walk out and the clerk yelled at her, "Oh Maria you do have some mail today, I'll get it in just a second." Maria heart was beating ninety to nothing, she knew who she hoped it was from. When the clerk handed it to her tears came to her eyes as she saw that it was from Mr. Wilson. He had sent money for her and Juan to come to the border crossing this border crossing by bus this Saturday morning. When she read this she could not control herself, her emotions got the best of her and she cried all the way home hoping that she could find him there or even the bag still there.

When she open the door and he was not there she ran to the bedroom to see if his bag was still there. She knew if they were there he had not left yet. Maria went ahead with the laundry and started fixing supper knowing that Juan would be home sometime today with his clothes still there. Maria had finished with supper and just started to sit down by herself to eat when Juan walked through the front door. He went to the bathroom to wash up for supper. Maria did not question him on where he had been she just fixed his plate as she always had with one exception this time. She had placed the letter she had received in his plate for him to see and for him to read.

He picks up the envelope and saw whose name that it was from tears started coming down his cheeks. "I just did not have faith in him mom, thank you lord thank you. Juan turned to his mom then and said,

"Can I run and tell Rio mom he needs to know the good news"

"not until you eat first then you have to start packing your clothes. You know that you are going to be there for quite a while" Maria said before she could say slow down eating his food it was already gone and he was headed for the door to go see Rio. They talked for a while then Mr. Diaz wished Juan the best and told him they would be leaving in about two weeks to loo0k for them a job in the city. Juan told Rio that maybe someday he could come to the states that maybe he would have a job for him. Then Juan turned and walked away6 from one of his best friends that he ever had never to see him no more.

Juan goes back home and finds the largest bag he could find to put his clothes in, all the time Maria telling him how to clean them when they needed washing, and for him to find someone to iron them for him. She then tells Juan where he was going to meet him at the crossing at, then she said that Mr. Wilson would have all of his papers for him to go across the border. Then warned him not to mess with other people at the crossing until Mr. Wilson got there to get him.

It was breaking Maria heart all the time she was helping him get ready to leave, but she knew that it was for the best for them, now she could remain there and not have to leave and look for work. She knew now he would not have to cross the desert by his self. "Mom a don't you think it would be best if you go to the crossing with me, but she told him that she would just see him off at the bus station in the morning but he tell Mr. Wilson thanks for everything that he is doing that she to maybe one day would see him also.

The next morning they make their way down to the bus station early enough for her to get him a bite to eat before he boarded it. As they were sitting there eating their food Juan looked over to her and said "Mom I will send you money every week at the store, you just be there to get it, and when I can will find a way to get you there with me. Everything will be ok, you will not have to work no more, and I will be the one doing the work". As the bus pulls up Maria says "Son remember your mom, come and see me when you can when you can find the time as tears come streaming down her face as she kiss Juan on the forehead "By mom I will see you before long, I hope "as he steps on the bus and sits by the window so he could see her as the bus begins to pull away. This time he has a feeling in his heart as the tears began to swell in his eyes. He waves until he could see her no more.

The two hours trip to the crossing was to Juan twelve hours long not knowing what was ahead. When they finally arrived at the crossing, Mr. Wilson was there waiting for him to start across so he could give him his work visa and a permit to stay for one year, then it could be renewed at that time.

On the trip to Mr. Wilson's home he explained tom him what he and Mary had talked about. You will go to college at night and work during the day until he learned the business from the labor stand point. He told him that a great niece was coming from Colorado to handle the office business and all he was going to do was to take care of the work force for the first year or so. Then the next year he was to learn what to plant to make the most profit and still handle the work force as well. He then asked Juan if he thought he could handle it and the reply was, I do believe that I can handle it.

When they arrived at Mr. Wilson's home, there was a car in the drive way. It was the niece that he had talked about on the road. She was a year older than Juan but she already had her college in business over with. When they went into the house they found Mary and her talking about the business already. So Brandon introduced Juan to her and told her about him and the part that he was going to play in the business and that they were to work together and see if they could handle it within the next few years. Brandon then told him that the young lady's name was Katie Young. Then he told the two to go in the living room while Mary fixed them something to eat, and get acquainted with other then they would go to the factory and let them look around and see what they did there at the work place.

When they sat down at the table all the talk was on the business and then after they were through the two young people made Mary and Brandon go in the living room so they could clean up the kitchen. When all was finished in the kitchen and all was sitting around talking Brandon asked Juan why he did not took Katie down to the warehouse and show her the work and how to get down there for Monday morning.

They both agreed as they left. Brandon and Mary how they thought this was best for their business. They both wanted to retire in the next five years but they wanted the business to continue on when they left it.

Monday morning came around and the two young people were already on the job talking with the other workers as to what was involved in the job they were supposed to do. It was not long before Brandon showed up and took each around to their places to work and told the workers there to show Katie what she was supposed to do. Katie went into the office and Juan went to the fields to work with the laborers.

Things went well for the first couple of months. Juan was in college at night and working in the fields during the day. Brandon kept an eye on Juan for the first month or two and saw that he was getting a little depressed by his mother not being there. He had been sending his mom the money that he made each week by Mr. Wilson, that way he knew that she would be getting it.

Brandon had already been working on a plan for his mother to come to the states and live in one of their rent houses. He had been talking to her by letter almost every week and he had not told Juan a thing about it. He knew that he would be a different worker if he had his mother there.

One Thursday he asked Juan if he could handle the business by his self that day because he had some business somewhere else. Both Juan and Katie said they could take care of it. Katie said she would drive Juan home that day from work.

The next day was payday for the workers and it was already taken care of, all they had to do was to hand each one their envelope that had their money in it. When the work was over for the day the men had gathered at the door of the warehouse to get their pay.

Name by name each was called and Katie handed it to Juan and he would hand it to the person and thank him for the weeks work.

Finally there was one left. Katie called the name of Jason Everett She handed it to Juan to give to him, but he drew it back when he saw who it was. "I believe you owe me four dollars from awhile back "Juan said as he took the four dollars out of the envelope and then handed it to him.

Jason said "I don't owe you nothing"

"You don't remember taking the money from the person at the corner store that day while two of your buddies held him and you beat him up for it. That was me. Now do you want the police to come and settle this or do you want to leave it as is." Juan said "no just take the four dollars and let it go." Jason said as Juan handed it to him. Then as Juan turns away he said "I still owe you something yet" he turns in a fast motion and lands his right hand on the cheek and nose of his face. "That is just one of those licks you gave me a few months ago" as he reached down to pick him up off the ground. "Do I need to call the police to decide this also?"

"No that's alright" he said as they turned to walk away from each other, Juan turns and says "I will see you Monday morning bright and early for work won't I' " He just throws up his hand as if to say ok. After closing the warehouse, the two headed to the Wilsons house. When they arrived Mary and Brandon met them and the drive way, he looks at Juan and said to him, "you do not live here no more, you will be staying at the house with the green shutters across the street" as he pointed down the block to the house. All Juan thought of was the fight, what had he done wrong, all these things he thought of as he started down the street to that house. He was wondering if he was going to send him back to Mexico what had he done.

As he reaches the walk of the house he sees a lady standing inside the house, so he goes to the door and knocks and hear some calls "come in" He enters the front door and then sees his mom standing there in the middle of the room with tears in her eyes. By this time Mary, Katie and Brandon had come over to see the commotion. Juan did not have the words to say to Brandon, all he could do was grab him in a big hug and say thank you. Brandon said "I will see you Monday morning at the warehouse, Katie will pick you up". "Thank you sir" Juan Replied

Monday morning the men were all gathered at the door to get their orders for the day. Brandon looked at the men and when he came to Jason he looked at how black and blue his face was and then said "What happened to you Jason" A little misunderstanding was all it was' he replied

Juan spoke up and said "If he gets behind today I will help him keep up". Then the men turned and walks toward their work. Then Juan walks over to Jason puts his arm around his neck and said "truly this is the land of the free and the brave.

RAY SOWELL

2800 E old oak

Poplar Bluff, MO. 63901

Printed in the United States
By Bookmasters